# THE TRACES OF BRILLHART

# THE TRACES OF BRILLHART

## HERBERT BREAN

**WILDSIDE PRESS**

*For Helen E. Brean with love.*

Published by Wildside Press LLC.
www.wildsidebooks.com

# THE EARLY TRACES

"My dear fellow," said Sherlock Holmes as we sat on either side of the fire in his lodgings at Baker Street, "life is infinitely stranger than anything which the mind of man could invent. We would not dare conceive the things which are really mere commonplaces of existence."

—Conan Doyle: *A Case of Identity*

# CHAPTER 1

*One Night, A Little Late*

I first knew Achille Robert Sinclair III for about two months, when we were both fourteen years old. That puts it back a little more than twenty years. My father had died and my mother and I moved to Columbus, because she had a brother there who could help us a bit, and presently I was introduced into the high school and enrolled as a freshman. This was after the spring semester had started and a thoughtful teacher made a point of finding out where I lived and introducing me to a boy who lived not too far away, so I'd have a friend. That was Archie Sinclair, as he got to be known later.

At the time he was known by his full first name, which is French and was so pronounced: *Ah—sheel.* Perhaps you can imagine what the other boys did with that, especially since the bearer of it was a gawky youngster with bad coordination, pipe-stem legs, and a chinless, eager, thick-spectacled face.

For the best part of two months Archie and I walked to school almost daily and he asked me over to his house quite a lot; he was a lonely, friendless boy. I asked him over to my uncle's too, but that wasn't very good because my uncle ran a truck garage which was right behind the house and quite often the drivers' language got a little frank. Not seriously; my aunt wouldn't have put up with that. Just profane for Archie. He was that kind of boy.

Archie lived in a house which was not enormous but after you got in it you realized it was bigger than the neighborhood average and much more expensive. There were oil paintings with lights illuminating them even in the daytime, and often a fire in the library fireplace and always a maid around someplace. Usually she brought us cookies and milk. Archie had a room with all sorts of things in it—snowshoes and skis, two chemistry sets, a lot of books, a saxophone he played with fair success, and assorted baseball gloves and footballs. Except for the saxophone, he never used these things much. Occasionally we took gloves and a ball out in the big back yard and tried to play catch, but he never knew what to do with them; maybe it was his eyes, which were weak and blinky.

Other times we stayed in the house and fooled around with the chemistry sets or talked about the books we liked. But that wasn't very good either, for while in school Archie had a great inferiority attitude and was quiet and timid, when he got home, where he could tell the maid what to do or command all his games and radio and chemistry sets, he got a little overbearing. Youngsters sense the meaning of these things fast and I soon realized that he was an unfortunate boy—spoiled, ineffectual and wistful. But realizing that didn't make him any better company.

Then March came and with it warm weather and baseball, and I tried out for a freshman team and made second base. After that, between homework and baseball, I didn't have any time for Archie and we lost track of each other. Before school ended that summer he disappeared and they said he had been sent to Europe. He wasn't around the following fall and I forgot him.

A few years ago a bunch of us came back on a Sunday night from a weekend out on the Island and stopped at this girl's apartment for bacon and eggs. Someone got fooling around on the piano, and I noticed that the sheet music included a song called "A Dollop with a Trollop," which was quite popular then. I also noticed that the composer was Achille Robert Sinclair III, and I knew I was hearing from my one-time friend. But that dropped from my mind too, and Archie Sinclair stayed forgotten until this recent night, twenty years after I last saw him. This is when the story really begins.

\* \* \* \*

After spending considerable time in this business, I've learned a few things and one of them is that the best thing you can do at the end of each day is to go over your notes and type them up. After a long session of interviewing, you are likely to feel that tomorrow will be time enough. It isn't. If you go over your notes soon after you make them, you remember little things you had no chance to write down at the time—the lilt of a phrase, exactly how someone looked when he did something; in brief, the sharp, telling detail that makes the ultimate article eloquent, if it is ever going to be.

That is why I was sitting in the office on this February night, hunched over a typewriter some four hundred feet above the neon glow of midtown Manhattan, which was intermittently visible through the high-flown gusts of snow whirling outside the window. I'd started work at 7:30 that morning at the Medical Center. I had spent the day with a courteous, very intent Chinese doctor who, in the opinion of his peers, was closer to achieving the restoration of life to a newly dead body than anyone had yet managed to be.

I was going to write an article about this for the magazine I work for and I knew toward the end of the day that what I was seeing and learning was going to make the main part of the story. That was why I was so anxious to get it all on paper—while I could still remember just how the three little rhesus monkeys had looked and how one of them, two hours after he had surely died, had opened his blank eyes and extended that tiny hand. It had twitched and the miniature movement had been hopeful, but uncannily frightening. Life had somehow supplanted death, an eerie reversal. When I left, there was still a chance he might live for the next twenty-four hours at least, even though he had been dead for two.

So I sat before a typewriter and the gooseneck reading lamp that illuminated it, trying to remember each detail, and trying to forget that because of a girl named Twit-Twit I had not paused for dinner or even a sandwich. I looked at my wrist. It was 10:40. I was seventy minutes late, for I had said I would be there at 9:30. There were six more pages of hieroglyphic notes to plow through and transpose into orderly typescript. And I was hungry.

I plowed on. It was a quiet place to work; the only sound except for the typewriter's sporadic rattle was the wet snow's whisper at the window and an occasional crack of the pane when a gust hit it. Aside from the pool of illumination cast by my lamp, the only light on the entire thirty-second floor was the glow of the night light near the elevators down the hall. I thought of Twit-Twit and the Dolans, whom I was meeting at Eddie Condon's. And how they were sitting over drinks and probably food as well, or at least were where they could order it. In any case, they would be listening to some good music.

I got up impulsively and walked down the dark hall to the water fountain, drank long, and came back. As I did, I heard a scuffle of footsteps in the other hall at the other end of the floor—the building policeman, prowling. And wondering what an idiot like myself was doing up here at this time of night when the rest of the town was beginning a relaxing weekend.

As I worked on, I began feeling resentful. You would think Twit-Twit might get a little worried. She could at least call and see if I was still here. After all, an elevator could have dropped, or I could have been hit by a taxi. But the phone did not ring. The building policeman kept walking around, checking empty offices. I heard him stumble as he went down the nearby stairs to the floor below.

I finished another page of notes and thought how *quiet* it was. And dark, except for the one lamp. It occurred to me that perhaps Twit-Twit had called and left a message and the operator had never notified me because she wouldn't know I was here. I lifted the telephone and waited. The phone was quiet. So was everything else. The watchman was gone; the switchboard had long since given up. The wind rattled the window again suddenly, and still hoping that an operator might answer I looked out of it, waiting. That is how I saw the dark reflection in it. Someone was standing silhouetted in the dimly lit doorway behind me. He must have been standing there for quite a while, for I hadn't been typing for a couple of minutes, yet I had not heard him at all. It wasn't Tom Dolan, who might have come up looking for me, because Tom never stood anywhere silently. And it wasn't the building policeman. The reflection showed a coat and hat.

I sat still, phone to ear, repressing my first impulse to leap around and demand, "What the hell are you looking for?" But I began to feel mad at the alarm he was causing me. I studied the reflection in the dark window appraisingly. Either the glass distorted it or he was remarkably tall and thin.

I turned. He *was* tall and thin. I said, "Well?" and he came forward, sinuously, like a snake in a long black overcoat.

"Hello," he said. "Did I startle you? I didn't want to interrupt your phone call."

I took a breath and let it out. "Who are you looking for?"

He said, "William Deacon. Aren't you him—or he?"

Nobody calls me by my full name any more.

"Who are you?"

"Archie Sinclair." A thin, long hand swam into the lamp's pool of light offering itself to be shaken, a hand as clean and white as a cavern fish.

There was a wall light switch behind me and my fingers found it. "Well, I'll be damned," I said in the new flood of light. It was indeed Archie. I shook the hand, and associations came flooding back.

Friendship is a skill that I am poor at. It isn't that I undervalue friends. But I believe that most friendship is approximately one half interests and sympathies in common, which is what friendship should be. The other half is happenstance. If you are forced to spend three days with a stranger of reasonably decent tendencies on train or shipboard, you become "friends." For three days. But the human personality is dynamic, and two personalities continue being friends only so long as they maintain the same parallel relations to each other. That is why genuine lifelong friendships occur so seldom. Certainly it had not occurred between Sinclair and myself. Now we were strangers, long grown into heaven knew what different patterns, and yet constrained to observe a forgotten relationship with a semblance of cordiality.

"Hello, Archie," I said.

"I'm glad you remember me."

"Why shouldn't I? It's been a few years though. Sit down."

"Thanks." He removed the black Homburg and loosened the long black coat that gave him the look of a Balkan conspirator. He was still inches taller than I, and the nose was still a pallid thin peak between eyes that were squinting little knots behind the porthole-thick glasses.

"I'm really sorry to interrupt. I stood in the doorway, wondering whether to go away."

"Don't be silly. I'm curious as to how you found me, though. I'm seldom here at this time of night."

"I knew you'd be here," he said. "You had to be. It was time I got some sort of break."

*That's nice,* I thought. But I was a little bothered. Whatever had happened to him, I didn't want to listen to a tale of woe and self-pity, or be tapped for fifty bucks. I had work to do and what was left of an evening to get to.

I said, "What do you mean, exactly?"

"Well, I was walking past the building and I thought about you. I asked the night elevator man if you were in and he said he wouldn't know but that someone was still working up on that floor. I knew it had to be you."

"I don't get the logic."

He took out cigarettes, offered me one and, when I shook my head, lighted one for himself. It was late but he was going to stay awhile. Or so he thought.

"I've kept track of you over the years," he said. "I've read your articles all the time in the magazine. You get around a good deal, and I've noticed you seem to cover a lot of the crime stories and murder mysteries."

"Maybe you've also noticed I don't solve them."

"That's not the point. The point is—well, I won't bore you with the story of my life since we were kids."

*Thank heaven for that.* Now if Twit-Twit will only call and give me an excuse—

"For some few years I've been living here in New York. Quietly. I'm in music." I remembered the Dollop-Trollop thing. "I've written a few songs and one clicked."

"I know. Very clever tune."

"Thanks." He looked genuinely pleased. "Well, I said I'd try not to bore you. I also do arranging for television, and some off-Broadway shows. And I'm engaged to be married. But that's all beside the point. The point is that—that something has been happening to me lately."

"I see." Then, because I had to, "What, exactly?"

"That's why I thought of you. I don't have many friends—none I feel like confiding this to, if you know what I mean. And anyway, musical people aren't very good at practical advice. And I need practical help."

He hadn't changed much at that. He still felt entitled to call the maid whenever he needed something. I looked at my notes. Two pages left to go. I looked at my watch. After eleven.

"That's when I thought of you," he went on, and perhaps what I thought showed in my face; he came to the point rather fast. "Do you know of a guy named Brill Brillhart?"

"I guess not."

"He's a one-time band leader and A and R man—"

"A what?"

"A and R man. That stands for artist and repertoire. The guy in a recording company who decides what singer or what band will record what songs, and how the arrangements will be made."

"I should have remembered."

"Brill was a Jack-of-all-trades in music. He sang, he arranged, had a band—"

"And he was once on a TV panel show that had something to do with identifying tunes."

"You're right. You remember him. Sort of a big burly guy, quite handsome, really. He certainly appealed to women. Curly hair and all that."

"I remember what he looked like on TV. What about him?"

"Well." He looked at the window where the whispering snow was beginning to pile on the sill outside. "Brillhart's dead."

"Too bad."

"Sure. But he's—he haunts me."

I suppose it was the way he said it. For I knew instantly what he meant: not haunted in the way that a name or a face or a scent can haunt you. He meant haunt in the sense of a ghost. The return of the dead. That alarmed me. Not because I believe in ghosts but because I believe in neurotics. I'd rather not be confined with one at the top of a deserted building late at night.

"It began about a week ago," he said. "I was in P. J. Clarke's, having a drink. At the bar, before dinner. There were two fellows and girls at a table in the back. I heard one of the girls say, 'Brill? You don't mean Brill Brillhart?' And the other girl said, 'Sure. I got a wire from him today. He's been out on the Coast doing a musical. He's flying back tonight and wants me to have dinner with him on Friday.'"

Somehow that dry, querulous voice evoked the original scene. I could hear the girl announce her date, a little proudly.

"Well?"

"But he's dead, you understand," said Archie Sinclair. "Brillhart's been dead for two months."

"Then they were talking about another Brillhart. Why not? Brillhart's not a completely rare name. Or maybe he has a brother."

"Maybe he *had* a brother. But they were talking about the right one. I know. Look. It jarred me at the time but I thought like you do. It must be another Brillhart. Then the next night I went to a preview at Warner's. Inez Low was there."

"That dame who used to sing with bands?"

"Sure. Every band in the country. I don't know her at all but I've known of her for years. She was married to Brillhart once. In fact, I think she still is, though they've been separated quite a while. I heard her tell someone Brillhart was coming back to New York. She said he'd done this musical for

Twentieth Century for a lot of money and it seems he still owes her something on their separation settlement. I gather Inez wants to collect."

"So what the hell," I said.

"What do you mean, what the hell?"

"What's the point?"

"The point is what I told you. He's dead. I know he's dead. And these people talk like he's alive and is going to walk in the room any minute. Why should they?"

"That's easy. You're wrong."

"Wrong?"

"You've made a mistake."

"Oh, no, I haven't." He shook his head. "I've made no mistake. Brillhart's dead; that I know. But wait. Last night I took Mary to a party at Kim Winter's."

"You get around. I know of Kim Winter. Who's Mary?"

"The girl I'm engaged to. And I know Kim because I did some arrangements for her once. She sings, you know. After a fashion. Well, it turns out one of the girls who was at Kim's was the one I'd heard in Clarke's. The one who was having dinner with Brillhart on Friday. I think she's a singer, too. A kid."

"Friday's tonight."

"I know that. Do you realize what it means, Deac? That girl may be having dinner right this minute, somewhere in New York, with someone she thinks is Brillhart—"

"Oh, stop it," I said. "If she is, it *is* Brillhart. Fifty million Frenchmen can't be wrong. Look, Archie. It's good to see you. Let's have a drink soon. But in the meantime, I have some work to finish."

But he overrode me, and Archie was never a very forceful person. "Let me finish," he said. "This girl mentioned she was having dinner with Brillhart tonight and Kim Winter asked if the girl—her name is Pope or Poe or something like that—would give Brillhart his coat and hat. It seems he had been over at Kim's the night before and left them. Or so Kim said."

"So what?"

He was staring at the desk in front of him and he spoke in a dull voice. "The hat was an Alpine hat with lots of skiing buttons and a white brush. Gaudy. The coat is an old, beaten-up trench coat that was Brill's trademark, in a way. He used to wear that coat everywhere. I recognized it. It was his."

"Well, as you say, it's odd." All I wanted to do was get rid of him. "But it seems to me this especially proves beyond any doubt that you're wrong."

"Does it? Look, Deac. I was—" He suddenly looked up and his face was deadly white and pinched with a kind of held-in desperation. He stared at me doubtfully, making up his mind. "I'm going to tell you something I've never told anyone. I don't dare, and yet I've got to—to have someone know. I was at Brillhart's funeral, so to speak. And I know that the hat and coat were, you might say, buried with him."

"Really?"

"Really."

"And this was two months ago?"

"All of that."

"And now he's walking around, leaving the same hat and coat in places?"

"Don't even say it—God, it's insane! But he is. Maybe it's me who's insane."

Maybe so, I thought. I know that I am, to put up with this, at this time of night. One thing was clear: he was really disturbed and there was not much I could do about it. I thought of something.

"Instead of worrying about it, why don't you ask these people about their seeing Brillhart?"

"I don't dare."

"Why not?"

He didn't say anything, and my temper can get as short as anyone's, especially when I'm tired and hungry.

"Why not, damn it?"

He looked quietly, doggedly miserable.

Then I felt ashamed. "Look, this is very odd and I'd like to go into it further, maybe. But right now I really have to finish what I'm doing." And, with the usual pangs of remorse, "Why don't you wait for me while I finish? I'm going to join some friends at Condon's. If you want to come along, we'd be glad to have you. We could talk on the way." I threw him the evening paper.

"That's nice of you." He picked it up and gave me an odd little twisted smile. There seemed to be tears in his eyes; perhaps it was the glasses.

It was exactly midnight when I pulled the last sheet out of the typewriter, scooped up the others and my notebook, and said, "Let's go." Now that the work was over I could accept Archie's problem more casually. "What do you say?"

He stood up; it was like an old-fashioned, straight-edge razor opening itself. His face was pale and oddly set again. A long thin finger pointed to a page in the *Journal-American,* which is the paper I'd thrown him. But he said nothing. He looked at me and I looked at what he was pointing to. It was Dorothy Kilgallen's column and it said, "Friends are saying Brill Brillhart's new Hollywood score is so good that he is being considered for the next Feuer and Martin musical."

"I'm damned," I said.

Archie put on his coat and hat in silence. I switched out the lights. "Remember what I told you," he said. "The guy's dead. He died two months ago. He's *dead*. I know it."

* * * *

Going down in the elevator we were silent. For the first time I was beginning to think seriously of what he had said. I looked at him. He didn't *seem* wacky, exactly. What he said was crazy, but the way he said it wasn't.

I signed us both out and at Fifth Avenue we flagged a northbound cab.

"Tell me one thing," I said when we were in it. "You know this guy is dead, you say. You were at his funeral. Okay. If you know he is dead, why don't other people know it?"

The lights in Saks' windows flashed across his face, showing the stubborn set of the little wedge-like chin. "I can't say right now."

I said, "According to you, half of New York is walking around seeing him. Dining with him and hearing about him. Even bringing his coat to him. You say he's dead. How do you know? When everyone else knows he's alive?"

The cab squealed into Fifty-sixth Street. Archie pointed to the cab driver's back. "Later."

"Okay."

But I began to regret inviting him. It isn't always practical to feel sorry for people.

* * * *

When I had paid off the cab, he said, "Look—I can't tell you why I know he's dead because it isn't my secret."

"Okay, Archie, okay! I take it you didn't kill him."

"Oh, *no*!" But the anxious way he said it certainly killed the joke, not that it was one. "There's a good chance I can explain that part of it in a few days or so."

I have a nasty way of swinging from politeness to rudeness, and I'm not necessarily proud of it. Or of what I said now. "Take all the time you want. Just don't ask for help until you're willing to give some."

"Honestly..." he began miserably.

We went into the club.

# CHAPTER 2

## *A Matter of Leakage*

Condon's is a nice place anytime. On a cold and snowy night, after a long and difficult day, it's a little better than that. Twit-Twit and the Dolans were at a table near the band and I performed introductions and Eddie gave up a beat on the guitar to wave hello. When the waiter had come and been told, I said, "Well, how've you all been?" and Betsy Dolan said, "Fine."

Betsy Dolan is a girl, if that is the word, who is not as young as she once was. She would not, as the saying goes, leave you a great deal of change from a fifty-dollar bill. But she has black hair and a wonderfully exasperated manner, eyes that are never exasperated at all, and a very trim figure. The Dolans knock around in some of the circles that Twit-Twit and I do, and occasionally when the evening gets late enough and I have had enough to drink, I start making passes at Betsy. She never gets mad, her husband never minds, and I never get anywhere. It's a beautiful relationship.

Right now her husband said, "We're not fine at all. We're terrible."

"Terrible?"

"I haven't told anyone, Deac, but I'm not long for this world." He was staring at his glass. Tom is a big guy with a nice sense of humor, and a long, sad face that can make even something as melodramatic as that sound real.

"Oh, God," Betsy said. "He's going into it again."

Archie said, "Something wrong?"

"Oh, it's nothing really." Tom Dolan sighed. Then I knew everything was really all right.

"Tell them and get it over with," Betsy said. But her eyes crinkled with amusement. She has astonishingly blue eyes. The waiter put the drinks around and the whiskey tasted good. The band rode out on "Lady Be Good" and they were wonderfully and solidly together, and I began to feel all right.

"It began this morning," Tom Dolan said into that great quiet that you get after a good last chorus. He sipped thoughtfully. "Strange. This morning. And it seems like it was only last week."

"Oh, for Christ's sake," said Betsy.

Twit-Twit's smile was wise. "They went to a wedding," she told me. "This afternoon."

"Champagne," said Tom. "God, how I hate champagne."

"You should have started hating it earlier," said his wife. "Like at the reception."

"But what about your health?"

Tom turned to me. "Yes. There's that, too. I'll tell you about that. It began this morning. In the tub."

"The tub?"

"I took a bath."

"He takes baths," his wife explained. "Every February. It's sort of a hobby with him."

That must have been quite a wedding, I thought. Twit-Twit was smiling at me. She has blue eyes too, but they are a little greenish-blue and sardonic, and usually they see more than they should.

"And so?"

"Well, there I am," Tom said. "Lying in the tub. Prone. Or is it supine?"

Archie was listening intently. "If you were on your back you were supine," he said.

Tom turned and looked elaborately at Archie as if he had just sat down. "Thank you," he said, surprised. "Thank you. So there I am. Supine. And you know what? The water is almost covering my stomach. Almost but not quite. You know what I mean, Deac?"

"I get it."

"Good. You get it. Now get this. I am lying flat on my—or anyway, supine, as our learned friend here says. So the water is almost deep enough to cover me, but not quite. So you know what? Well, a little water happens to slosh over my stomach when I move. You know? So it covers me or anyway it covers my stomach for a moment. And you know what? Some of it sort of stays in my navel—you know? After all, I have a navel."

"Of course he does," his wife said. "He's got everything. God, what a dreamboat!"

"Shut up. You know what I mean, Deac? Your navel is a sort of depression in your belly. Like a cup."

"I know. I have one too."

"Another dreamboat," said Betsy. "This is my night." Twit-Twit's eyes were laughing.

"You know what I mean?" Tom asked.

"Sure," I said. "But I like to think of mine as a chalice. I'm kind of reverent, of course."

"You sure are."

"God," Betsy said simply. "Where's the waiter?"

Archie looked puzzled. At least his mind was off his troubles.

"Well, now get this, Deac. Get this. This is the crux of the matter."

"The chalice," Twit-Twit said.

"Chalice...crux...what am I doing? Saying Mass? Now look. So a little water collects in this depression formed by my navel—remember, I'm in my bath. Right? It's like a little sort of pool. Landlocked, so to speak. Right? And you know what? Well, pretty soon the water disappears."

He sat back like a scientist who has finally completed a two-hour refutation of Einstein.

"Well?" Twit-Twit said. Over her shoulder I saw Condon standing over a table near the bar, talking to some people. I wanted to talk to him.

"Well," Tom echoed. "How can you be so calm? Don't you realize the significance of what I just said?"

"No."

But Archie nodded.

"He gets it," Tom said, pointing to Archie. "He understands! You're the understanding type! What's your name again?"

"I can't take any more," Betsy said. "I just can't. Deac, get the waiter to bring double tranquilizers all around."

By really remarkable luck I got the waiter's eye.

"The water was draining into *me,*" Tom yelled exultantly. "That's where the water was going! My navel *leaks!* Can you imagine? I've got a leaky navel."

People at other tables were looking around.

"That's impossible," Archie said. But when Tom turned on him indignantly, he added, "Of course, I suppose anything is possible."

"Possible! Look, want me to give you a demonstration?" He unbuttoned his jacket and began unbuttoning his shirt.

"Tom Dolan! Are you working up to a divorce?" Twit-Twit and I were laughing. Archie looked uncertain, then he began to laugh.

"Tell the waiter to bring some water," Tom said loudly. "Sterile, of course. And body temperature. I'll show you. You know what? I think I've invented a new way to drink."

"And that's just what you need," said his wife. "Button your shirt."

Eddie had left the table he was talking to. There was quite a girl at it. She was blonde but not in the ordinary sense. The hair was short—chrysanthemum-cut, I think you call it—and the face animated and puckish. Looking at her, you recognized, not someone you've seen in movies or television, but rather someone you knew you were going to see. I got up. "Back in a moment," I said. "Meanwhile, be prepared, men. Keep your navels dry."

Somebody was having a steak at a table I walked past and it smelled wonderful. I remembered I hadn't ordered food.

Eddie said, "Hi. Where have you been?"

"Working. Days on end. Buy you a drink."

"No. You have one."

"I've got one at the table. What I really want is some information."

"So?"

"You know a guy who died recently named Brillhart? He was a singer, and song writer—"

"I know him. When did he die?"

"You didn't know he was dead?"

"Of course, the obituaries are not my favorite form of reading matter. But I never heard—hey, wait a minute. What are you talking about? Just tonight someone was saying Brillhart was back from the Coast after writing a musical out there. When did he die?"

"Who said it?"

"I don't know. I was talking to someone at a table—"

Someone yelled, "Hey, Eddie," and at the same time a bartender waved to him.

"Then tell me one thing. What kind of guy was he?"

"Well, I'll tell you," Eddie said. "There aren't very many people I'd pay this big a compliment to. But Brillhart was the biggest bastard I've met since I came to New York. That was in 1928. In this business that's a long time."

"In any business. Was he a good composer—or singer?"

The bartender yelled, "Hey, Eddie!"

The pianist finished "I Got It Bad and That Ain't Good" and went into, of all things, "Chinese Honeymoon." I said, "I haven't heard that one for a while."

Eddie said, "Nor me. He goes tonight. Well, I'll tell you. Brillhart could sing. I'll say that. And he wrote a couple songs that were popular. I always wondered, frankly, whether he wrote them or just promoted them for some poor slob who couldn't get to a publisher himself—you know what I mean?"

"How old a guy?"

*"Eddie!"* The bartender was getting mad. I like a place where the help bawls out the boss.

"How old was he?"

"Why do you keep saying *'was'*? He *is*. He's alive—far as I know. He's about thirty-seven, going on forty-two. Handsome guy, I'll say that. Big. Curly hair. Blond. Dashing fellow, you might say." Eddie's voice took on an English lilt.

"Eddie, God damn it!" The bartender was waving a check that needed an okay.

"Come 'round to the table. Tell me why he was a bastard. *Is* a bastard."

He tapped my elbow. "I gotta work. You'd better take that drink."

"Maybe I will."

I had it at the bar and it did something the first one hadn't done. When I got back to the table the band was beginning to assemble on the stand and Twit-Twit was telling how someone had insisted on taking her to the Stork Club, which she does not like, and what she told Billingsley when he tried to sit down at their table. It was sort of funny; Twit-Twit is pretty good at this sort of thing, and we all laughed.

Twit-Twit got her nickname partly because her last name is Twickenham, but mainly because when she was in a girls' school some of the other girls thought she was a little flighty and felt Twit-Twit fitted her. People have been making the same mistake ever since, so the name has stuck, and Twit-Twit has come to take a sort of pride in it. I think she would kill herself before admitting she's a Phi Beta Kappa and has a doctorate in chemistry. She also has an income and a divorce, and she likes staying up all night, talking to bartenders and musicians, and the guys who handle fish at the Fulton Market, beginning about 4:30 a.m.

I like her.

Right now it was nice to sit back and think about a steak sandwich and sip whiskey and water and watch the band go through the little asides and valve wigglings and soft drum rolls before they break out in the first number of a set. It occurred to me that it was very pleasant to do a hard day's work and then have the chance to relax pleasantly after it; Spenser had said something about it. I tried to remember. *Peace after toil, port after stormy seas.....*"

The band began and we all listened.

It was a couple of hours later, by which time I had eaten and was a little sharper all around, that Betsy's voice cut in on a cornet solo like a buzz saw hitting a nail.

"All right," she said, "All *right.* So you see something you like."

I looked at her and then at Tom. Tom had been looking to the left, past Archie Sinclair, past Archie's two untouched drinks, along to the table with the chrysanthemum-blonde girl. I concluded he had been looking for some time. Betsy sounded really mad, but Betsy's unreasonable at times, like any attractive woman.

However, Tom knows how to handle her. He just grinned. "I sure do see something I like. Who dat—anyone know?"

No one said anything but I noticed Archie look down guiltily and somehow I sensed that he knew who the girl was.

"I'd better get you home," Betsy said.

"Oh, for God's sake," said Tom. "I'm old enough to be her daughter. I mean, she's old enough to be my daughter." His bloodshot eyes were sleepy.

"That's what *I* mean," Betsy said. "Leave some money with Deac—this has been a busy day but you've had it." They left, Tom protesting loudly but good-humoredly. They really got along wonderfully well, I thought. When they were gone, I said, "Who's the blonde, Archie?"

He raised his head and smiled, wearily. "That," he said, "is the girl I heard saying she was having dinner with Brillhart tonight."

* * * *

After a minute, I said, "I'll be damned."

"Now you begin to realize how it haunts me."

"What's all this?" said Twit-Twit.

"He's not the guy with her, is he?"

"You're damned *right* he's not with her!" Archie said viciously. "I told you where he is!"

Twit-Twit didn't ask any more questions, but I could *feel* how she was listening.

"You think I'm crazy, eh?"

"Of course not. But I'm beginning to get sort of interested. What's the blonde's name?"

"It's Poe or something like that. I think she is trying to be a singer."

"I'll bet she goes a long way."

Twit-Twit said, "So do I. And you haven't even heard her sing."

"Don't be a Betsy. There's a reason for this."

"I'll try to care less. Hello, Eddie."

Condon had come up behind me.

"Sit down and have a drink."

"You have one with me." He sat down and gestured to the waiter. "This is me, Sal." The waiter nodded.

I said, "Eddie, who's the blonde crew-cut three tables over?"

He waited a moment to turn. Then, "That's Eulalia Pope. She's a kid singer, trying to get started. That's her brother with her. He's fronting for her. He offered to have her do a few numbers with the band. They're really trying."

"You didn't let her?"

Condon looked at me. Then he said, "I think Brill Brillhart's coaching her." I heard Archie's nostrils take in air.

*What the hell,* I thought. "I'd like to meet her."

"I'll take you over before the next set."

"You could say I'm thinking of doing a story on the tribulations of young singers."

"I won't need to. Any prayer of publicity will look good to her."

We talked for a while, then when Eddie said, "I got to get to work," we got up, and I leaned over to Archie. "Once and for all, you are sure—you really *know* of your own knowledge—that this guy is dead?"

The gnomish, almost chinless face that looked up at me wrinkled pathetically. "Darn sure."

"Nobody seems to have seen the obit."

Behind the telescopic lenses his eyes became hot with emotion. "Brillhart saw it."

At the other table Eddie explained things and when she heard I worked for a magazine I got a warm welcome. The blonde hair really was like a shaggy chrysanthemum but the face was pert and alert, and the black dress fitted like so much fresh paint. Her brother said I had to have a drink but I said no, and explained that I just wanted to ask a few questions, if she didn't mind, since I might do a piece on how tough it is for young singers to get started. She didn't mind.

Behind me, the band started with "Changes." I had to talk a little loud.

"I really don't know much about this sort of thing," I said. "I just have the idea that a story on how the big singers came up and how a lot of the young ones are getting started today could be of interest. Because it seems to me there is more competition than ever, and more ability required—"

"You're certainly right." The carelessly shaggy head shook itself carefully so as not to spoil its careless look. "It's a full-time job, what with appearances and voice lessons and recording dates. Of course, my records so far"—she smiled modestly—"have just been singing commercials."

"But for big agencies," her brother said.

"I can imagine. Tell me, Miss Pope, what would an average day be like for a young singer like yourself? Take today, for instance? What did you do today?"

Big eyes and a cute nose crinkled in thought; whatever else she was, she was all girl. "I know what you mean. Pictures of—well, a day in the life of, you call it. Right?"

I shuddered at the cliché and said, "Right."

"Well, I was up about ten. Frank and I had been over in Brooklyn, rather late, at this small club. I did a few numbers—for free, but it gets you exposure."

"Sure."

"We'll get paid," said Frank, with frowning confidence.

"So I slept later than usual this morning, and showered and had breakfast. And read *Variety*. And—let's see."

"Just a minute," said Frank. "We're talking about pictures—right?"

"Possibly."

"Well, if you have any ideas of getting pictures of Eulie getting out of bed, or in the shower, or anything like that—you don't get them."

"That's not what I had in mind."

I really had nothing in mind. But Frank's belligerence began to interest me. For a brother, he seemed very protective of his pretty sister—almost sexually jealous. And for a brother he didn't look much like her.

"Don't be silly, Frank," she said. "After breakfast I went to the studio and practiced voice, and then piano—there are two numbers in that new Rodgers and Hammerstein show I think fit my style. I had lunch with a girlfriend who's studying ballet and afterwards we shopped and then I went to my dentist's. He's getting ready to cap two of my teeth that show up badly when I open wide. That's important on television. Then home early because I had a dinner date."

"Anybody special?"

"Sort of. My voice coach." But the way she smiled and dropped her eyes made it more than a voice coach. Frank's face grew a little stony. "He's just back from Hollywood."

"Who is that?"

"I think you know him. He mentioned tonight that he knew this magazine writer, so I suppose you two may be friends. He's Brill Brillhart."

I'd never met Brillhart in my life. I'd never heard of him until tonight.

I said, "Oh, sure. Of course. And you two had dinner?"

"At that nice little place on Fiftieth just off Third—La Cloche d'Or. It's near Brill's apartment."

"Where's he living these days anyway?"

"Same place. He didn't give up his apartment in the Sweltering Arms when he left."

"The what?"

"All the apartments in the building have air conditioners and his is the only one in the whole building that doesn't work."

I knew La Cloche d'Or, so I took a chance. "Oh, yes. I think I know that building—on Fifty-second near Lexington."

"Fiftieth and Third—the northwest corner, I think it is."

"Let's get back to your day. What did you do after dinner?"

"Brill had someone to see about the sheet music for this musical he's written and so he took me home and then Frank and I came over here."

Frank cut in fast. "I'm managing Eulalia, in case you get the impression Brillhart is. We'd promised Condon she'd sing a few numbers, but her throat is a little raw and we had to beg off."

"I'm sorry," I said. "I'd love to hear you sing." I got up. "Look, if we decide to do this story, could I ring you sometime and arrange a detailed interview? And perhaps some pictures?"

She lit up like the Christmas tree in Rockefeller Center.

"You certainly can," she said. "But I'll go you one better. Tomorrow night we're having a little get together at Kim Winter's apartment. There'll probably be other young singers there to hear a run-through of Brill's new score. Sort of a preview. If you'd like to come—I know Kim'd love to have you—you would certainly meet some of the best new talent."

"Who will be playing the score?" I asked.

"Why, Brill, naturally," she said.

"I'd love to."

I walked back to our table feeling something like a detective. But also wondering what I was doing.

Twit-Twit had gone to the powder room. Archie said, "What did she say?"

I considered a moment. "Well, she claims to have had dinner with him tonight. Then he left to keep a business date."

His fingernail began making grooves in the tablecloth. "Are we all going nuts?" His voice was far down in his throat.

"Don't you think it's time you told me why you think he's dead?"

His head was so bent over that his chin was on his necktie. He shook his head.

"*How* do you know?" I said, pretending anger; I wasn't mad although I was beginning to get curious.

But that scared him. When he looked up, there were tears in his eyes. "Look, Deac, you're the only friend I've told about this. Honestly. Please don't push me right now. I told you, it isn't my secret and I swear to you that I am innocent of anything. I didn't kill him—"

"But somebody did?"

He looked miserable, and I knew something had slipped out.

"And you know about it."

He continued looking down. I waited.

"I'll tell you what I'll do," he said at last. "I want your help. I need it. I know Brillhart is dead and I'm the only one—well, almost the only one who does."

"Don't count me in on that—I don't know it!"

"I'm not counting you in. But I want you in. Because you know the ropes about—about crime and investigations and so on. And something very strange and unnatural is going on here. Now look, Deac."

Behind the thick glasses his eyes blinked sincerity at me. "In a few days something could happen that will make it possible for me to tell you everything. Will you do this? Will you be patient and stick with me and give me a hand during that time if I need it? In return I will deposit—well, say five thousand dollars in your name in any bank you want. When the thing that's going to happen finally happens and I tell you everything, if you feel that I have deceived you and involved you in anything disgraceful, you can keep the money. It's a sort of bond. Fair enough?"

"Oh, for the love of Mike! Lay off the five-thousand-dollar bit. Who do you think I am—and what can I do? I'm a magazine writer, not a private eye. Besides, it isn't that I don't believe you—"

"Maybe it isn't," he said doggedly. "But it isn't that you believe me either. Look, Deac. Believe this: I am the only man in the world who knows that Brill Brillhart is dead and also knows that either his ghost or some insane impersonator of him is going around New York right this minute, fooling everyone into thinking he's Brillhart."

"But you could be wrong."

"But I'm not wrong. I know what I'm talking about."

"Archie, that sort of thing is impossible. No one can impersonate another person to his intimate friends."

"I know that. And that's why I want you to help find out what's going on. Because something crazy is. You can use the five thousand deposit to draw on for expenses too, of course."

His family really left him well fixed, I thought.

"You're offering me a retainer?" I asked sarcastically. "Is that it?"

"Will you do it?" he asked.

"I won't take any retainer," I said. "And I don't intend to do anything about it until you tell me what you know about it."

The thin shoulders drooped. Twit-Twit was wending her way back from the powder room. She is slender and lissome, and when she wends she wends.

Then I thought of what would happen if I told him that Brillhart was going to play a sort of recital tomorrow night. Twit-Twit got back to the table.

"It *is* getting on," she said, "And as the Deacon you must open the church in the morning." It was an old, poor joke.

"I'll get a check."

* * * *

There was a cab waiting outside, but Archie said he'd walk. It wasn't snowing anymore and the night was clear; the city smelled clean and looked freshly frosted. "I'll call you," I told Archie. We all said good night.

"Now," said Twit-Twit when we were settled in the cab, "what's this about? What did you do to your friend?"

"What do you mean?"

"No static, my boy. When I came back to the table he looked like an eight-year-old kid who'd lost his jackknife."

I told her the outline, in a low voice because of the driver. When I had finished, she said, "I'd like to go to that party tomorrow night at Kim Winter's."

"I didn't say I was going."

"You don't have to."

"If you are waiting for an invitation, you must have forgotten that you already have a heavy date, one of long, long standing. That's what you said when I asked you to go to the fights with me."

Twit-Twit said, "You're going to try to locate Brillhart anyway," as though I had not said anything. "And you'll try to find where he lived, in case he's dead."

"Maybe I will," I said. "But if I do anything at all about this, it will be just to call Brillhart up. I imagine he's in the telephone book. That won't be much trouble."

"Go to hell."

I put my arm around her and she closed her eyes and put her head on my shoulder. I kissed her, twice. Suddenly she drew away and began redoing her lipstick energetically. Sometimes Twit-Twit can read my mind.

"I shouldn't have let you keep me out so late," she said. "I have to be up at dawn. But it *was* fun."

"Have a big time with your date," I said.

"Call me for Sunday brunch."

"I'll look at my engagement book."

But I knew I would call her, and I knew that she knew it. And I didn't mind.

# CHAPTER 3

### *A Walk on the East Side*

I slept late.

When I woke it was a little after one and I stayed there, drowsy and comfortable, for another half hour. Then I turned on the bedside radio and listened to the news, and thought a little, and got up and heated coffee. I took a cup back to bed and sipped it and thought some more—about Archie and his problem, but also about pleasant things, like Twit-Twit and what Pee Wee Russell had done to "The Blues in B-flat" last night and what I would do about dinner tonight.

That's what I like about weekends—the beginning. The feeling that so much time stretches in front of you, and you don't have to do anything with it, and can afford to waste some. Maybe it's the result of working constantly against deadlines.

Finally I got up, showered, and put on flannel pants, shirt, and tennis shoes, made breakfast, and took in the paper. By the time I felt like moving away from the table it was three o'clock, and I was getting curious.

I looked for Brillhart in the Manhattan phone book and found there were no Brillharts listed. I thought awhile, then called the magazine and asked the girl in the morgue—you know that on a news publication that means reference library, of course—to look up Brillhart in the files. I also asked if she'd look through our collection of Manhattan phone books. When she came back she said that Brillhart was unlisted in phone books going back through 1952 and that his file consisted of two news clippings, one ten years old telling about how he was writing a show with Rudolf Jersey, the famous song writer, and the other about how some tailor had sued him for an old bill.

I said, "No obituary notices?"

"None at all."

"Thanks, Amy."

I thought a little more and called Dr. Wu, the scientist I had spent the day with yesterday.

In a moment his polite, Oriental voice said, "Hello, Mr. Deacon."

I felt like an oaf. "Doctor, I'm sorry to bother you. Especially with a damn-fool question."

"Mr. Deacon, a scientist cannot expect a journalist to understand all the nooks and crannies of his own specialty. Otherwise, journalists would be scientists, and scientists would be out of jobs." He chuckled.

"I doubt that. But here's the question. Doctor, has anyone done any serious, practical work on the resuscitation of human beings?"

"How do you mean that?"

"I mean—I don't know what I mean. I know it sounds idiotic, but has anyone, anywhere, brought dead humans back to life, even experimentally? In the way that you yourself have revived monkeys and mice, for example?"

"No. Not in the sense I think you mean."

"I've heard the Russians—"

"So have I. But hearing is one thing, and scientific documentation another. As you know, it is quite a problem getting reliable scientific information out of Russia."

"Then the only work done has been on animals?"

"Yes, virtually, as far as I know. And little of that. May I explain, Mr. Deacon, that the problem is one of tissue change, to put it in a general way. Above all, in brain tissue. The heart is usually regarded as the vulnerable organ, but the heart is astonishingly strong and tough. It has the will to live, and when it stops it wants to resume beating. That is why it responds so well to massage, when it stops during an operation. But the massage has to begin at once and the chief reason is the brain. Denied the oxygen that the heart pumps to it, the brain dies within minutes, regardless of what is happening to the rest of the body."

"Then there is no record or scientific possibility—I don't know how to put this—of a human being being brought back to life after having been dead for days, or even weeks?"

"Well...not a matter of days or weeks, surely. There was a case that may interest you which was reported a few years ago in the A.M.A. *Journal.* (*June 2, 1956, *Journal of the American Medical Association, pp.* 434-436). As I recall the details, a medical man, a doctor, who had been visiting a patient in a mid-western hospital was leaving the building around noon when he suddenly fell over dead of a heart attack. He was a man in his sixties with a coronary history. However, he was rushed to a nearby operating room and a team worked over him, first by cardiac massage to keep the heart pumping, artificially, and then by electric shock to get it going on its own. This went on for forty minutes, during which the man was, to all purposes, dead. At one point no heart sound was detectable at all.

"Yet after forty minutes they got the heart started. The patient was again alive. Next morning, a semblance of consciousness returned, and by noon the patient could speak words. Even the following day his thoughts and words were still disconnected and confused. He never regained any memory of the crucial thirty-six hours of his heart attack. But he recovered, and fully. There are other cases on record, of course."

"But no one has ever—" I stopped.

Again I heard the dry chuckle. "You mean, are there no mad scientists these days, reviving corpses?"

I laughed. "I guess that's exactly what I mean."

"I'm afraid the tissue change involved precludes it. First, one would have to find a way to preserve tissue in every way, for the subsequent resuscitation."

"Which is impossible." I really felt like a damned fool.

This time there was a long pause. "In my experience, nothing is impossible to nature and science."

We both thought for a time across the silent wire. "Suppose," I said, "a man were somehow resuscitated after being dead some days. Would he be the same person—psychologically, I mean? Have the same moral values and personality and all that?"

This time the pause was very long.

"I do not know," said Dr. Wu finally.

In saying, "Thanks. Good-by, doctor," I found my throat rather dry.

But I no longer felt like a damned fool.

* * * *

I got dressed and took a bus uptown. I got off at Fiftieth Street. It was a nice Saturday, clear and cold but the sky was a deep-blue background for the gray spires of St. Pat's and the westbound planes from LaGuardia, glinting silver in the sun, droned cheerfulness. There were girls with nice legs on Madison and a few shop windows worth looking into and there was also the knowledge that what I was doing didn't really matter because the whole thing was ridiculous and would be explained sooner or later. Above all, it was an earned day off.

I walked to Third and Fiftieth, studying the buildings. There were only three apartment houses in the whole block and only one had the tiers of air conditioners in its windows that answered Eulalia's description. I walked to Second to make absolutely sure, came back and went into the neat vestibule. There was the usual panel of buttons and printed names, and polished brass letter boxes. One of the names opposite a button was Brillhart. I pressed the button.

Nothing happened.

I pressed again. Still no salutation.

I looked in the letter box; no mail for Brillhart. Someone had collected it, then, unless he had no correspondents at all. That was hardly likely. I pressed a button marked "Custodian."

The lock buzzed and I walked in. It was dark after the sun-brilliance outside and it was a moment before I saw the dark passage leading away from the several steps down. A man's head projected from a door in the passage. It said, "Yes?"

"I've been ringing Mr. Brillhart's bell. He doesn't answer. I was wondering whether he's in town."

"Can't say."

I walked down and he came out the door, holding a napkin. He was a squinting, tousle-haired caricature wearing an unbuttoned vest and the exasperated air of caretakers.

"You mean that you don't know? Or you're not allowed to say?"

"Both."

"I see. Well, I owe Mr. Brillhart some money. I wanted to pay him. Can I leave it here with you?"

"How much?"

"Three hundred dollars. But I want him to get it right away."

"No, sir." The hair shook energetically. "I can't take no responsibility for no three hundred bucks."

"Why not?"

"He might not be back again for a couple weeks. What do I do with it meanwhile?"

"Hasn't he been around for a couple weeks?"

"I haven't seen him for two months. I got a note from him a week or so ago enclosing last month's rent and saying he'd be back soon. And he has been. I have to check the apartments every so often when the people are away and the last couple times I went into his, things had been moved around a little. Like the music on the piano. He's been in and out."

"I see. Well, thanks—I can understand your not wanting to take the responsibility for the money." I tried to sound sympathetic. "When you see him, will you tell him Mr. Pollock was here?"

Sudden hope crossed the crafty face. A hunch is a sometime thing. I found two dollar bills and handed them over. "Thanks much for your trouble. I'm afraid I disturbed your lunch."

"Oh, that's all right, Mr. Pollock. No trouble at all. I'll sure tell him." Then something else came into his face. "Ah...none of my business of course but is—is Mr. Brillhart in any kind of trouble?"

I stopped pulling on my gloves. "Not that I know of. Why do you ask?"

"Well...like I said, it's none of my business. Don't get me wrong. But Mr. Brillhart's lived here over three years now and no one's inquired for him.

Then maybe a month or more ago a girl came and asked about him and his apartment. Then another. Darned pretty girls, too. Then just a little while ago another one comes. And now you."

"Today? The same pretty girl?"

"No. Another one. She just left a couple minutes before you rang."

It might be nothing, of course, or just coincidence. But he said no one had inquired about Brillhart for three years. Now people were doing it.

"What did she look like—cute? Nice?"

"The last one?" He looked aggrieved. "How can you tell these days? She had a build, I'll say that for her. She was wearing a fur coat—mink, I guess. And she was kind of pretty. She—well, now, *by Gawd!*"

He was looking beyond me up the hall, gaping. "There she goes!"

A girl, slender despite the fur coat, was tripping across the small foyer to the front door. Very chic.

"What is this?" the caretaker bawled. He pushed me aside and ran up the stairs to the foyer. He grabbed the girl by the elbow. "Where *were* you? Up in that apartment? I told you he wasn't there if the bell didn't answer."

The girl turned on him regally. "I *beg* your pardon?"

I said, "'Unhand me, villain' is the usual line."

She studied me without surprise but a lot of contempt. "Where have you been?" the caretaker insisted. He looked like an elderly terrier.

"I simply went up to Mr. Brillhart's apartment and knocked."

"Why?"

"It occurred to me that the bell might not be working."

"It took a long time for you to find out whether it was or not," the caretaker said suspiciously. "At least ten minutes."

"I'm the thorough type," she said. "And if you don't take your hairy paw off my coat I'll scratch my initials all over your face."

"What *are* your initials?" I said.

"We're going upstairs," the caretaker said. He let go her arm but he looked more like a terrier than ever. "Sorry, Mr. Pollock. But I gotta make sure this dame didn't break in."

"I'd do that," I said. "And I think maybe Mr. Pollock"—I emphasized the name—"will go along, too. I'm curious."

"Why, sure."

We took the self-service elevator up to the third floor and the caretaker took out a passkey before one of the two doors in the small hall. He opened the door, stepped back and said, "You first, sister," and she walked in. I followed. The caretaker came in and put the passkey down on a table. I looked around curiously; this was Brillhart's apartment. The living room was to the left, plain and not looking specially lived-in. The caretaker said, "Mr. Pollock, would you keep an eye on her? I'm going to have a look-see."

"Sure thing."

To the girl he said, "Don't try anything, sister."

He went into the living room and looked around. I watched him, fumbling in my coat pocket meanwhile for my keys. I did not look at the girl but I said, "Don't try anything, sister."

The caretaker went to the door of what I gathered was a bedroom and looked in. I had keys in hand now and inspected them quickly, then unhooked one from the ring. It was the key to my own apartment, but I knew I had another someplace. I took a quick step to the table where he had put down the passkey, picked it up, and put mine in the same place. Sooner or later he must discover the substitution but if he didn't see me do it what could he prove?

He went on to what was apparently the kitchen. Without taking my eyes off him I whispered to the girl, "Keep your mouth shut." She whispered something back and it would destroy your faith in womanhood if I told you what it was.

The caretaker returned. "Everything *seems* okay," he said.

The girl said, "May I go now?" and added sarcastically, "Sir?"

The caretaker looked at me.

I said, "She tells me she's a friend of Brill's and she apparently knows some people he knows. I really think it's all right. That is, if there's nothing missing." I looked at her speculatively, and added, "I think she's just some sort of screwball."

The caretaker seemed a little relieved. "Well, there's nothing wrong, far's I can see." He picked up the key.

We went downstairs. At the door I said grandly, "When Brill gets back, tell him to call me, would you? He knows where."

"I sure will, Mr. Pollock."

"Thanks a lot. After you, miss." I swung open the front door.

"Thanks again, Mr. Pollock."

We reached the sidewalk.

The girl said, "Mr. Pollock, eh?"

"Why not? And what the hell are you doing here?"

"I just got curious," said Twit-Twit, "thinking about the story you told me. It's the kind of nutsy thing that's impossible. And therefore interesting. And I had to come over this way anyhow."

"Well, for God's sake stop getting curious. The whole thing is nutsy and Archie is nuttier than anyone. Keep out of it."

"And what are *you* doing here, if I am permitted to ask any questions at all?"

"It just might make a magazine story, you know."

Twit-Twit snorted expensively scented disgust. "Mr. *Pollock!* A pollock is a fish. You picked a good alias, at that."

We walked toward Lexington. Her shoulders seesawed independently under her coat and I could tell she was mad that I had had to rescue her, if rescue is the word.

"What got you so interested?" I said.

"I'll tell you why. I have a date tonight and he's going to be a bore. Almost as bad as last night's date except this one'll be on time. So in the meanwhile I thought I might stir up a little excitement for myself. You spoiled it."

"If I hadn't spoiled it, you might have wound up in the Seventeenth Precinct, trying to explain what you were up to."

"Shut up, you Irish slob."

"I'm glad tonight's date will be a bore. Mine won't."

"Are you really going to that party?"

"With lots of beautiful girl singers? You're darned right. And you can't come. But right now I'll buy you a drink."

"I don't want a drink. Tea."

"Tea! Do you realize the sun is setting? It's Martini lighting time in the valley."

"No. Tea. I had a dozen drinks last night. And after all, a girl's got to think of her figure."

We were crossing Lexington. "If you're having a busy afternoon," I said, "I'll be glad to think of your figure for half an hour or so, while you do something else."

Twit-Twit squeezed my arm. "You can be a pleasant slob at times. Though still basically a slob. Where'll we go?"

"There's always the Plaza."

"The Plaza."

A taxi came along.

* * * *

We had tea in the Palm Court. That is, Twit-Twit did—some sort of Chinese tea and cinnamon toast. I had a Sahara Martini.

She was quiet until after the toast came. Then she said, "Do you think he's alive?"

"Who?"

"Brillhart, you two-headed bastard."

"Why do you care?"

"*Do* you?"

"Well, I know how crazy it's going to sound," I said, "but I don't think he is alive. I think he's dead. I suppose that's why I'm going to the party tonight."

"You believe your friend Archie, then?"

"I do, to be honest, but I don't know why I do. He sure didn't explain anything. It's just that he sounded convincing. But don't think I won't get the story out of him."

She poured hot water into her teapot. "How about a masquerader?"

"That's silly. No one can masquerade successfully, like this."

"I suppose. But why do people keep seeing him?" Incongruously, I thought of the monkey's little hand.

"I don't know why. But they do."

"Yes," said Twit-Twit. "More than you think."

I looked at her.

She said, "Why do you think I was so interested in this today?"

"Okay. Why?"

"Last night after you dropped me off I got to thinking. That name Brillhart had rung a bell. Then I remembered. Monday night the Dolans and I were having dinner together, so Betsy and I picked up Tom at the studio after the seven-o'clock show. There was another show there, a musical, that was going on at eight and they were all having coffee and sandwiches and Tom introduced me to this girl who was in the musical—a singer. Not necessarily young."

"What was her name?"

"Low or Loewy, or something like that. She was talking about how her ex-husband had just made a lot of money in Hollywood and had paid her some dough he owed her under the separation agreement and so she had been able to get her fur coat out of hock. She was showing it off."

I could guess what was coming, and Twit-Twit nodded. Her eyes were dark with wonder. She said, "Afterward, when I asked Tom who her ex-husband was, he said it was a guy named Brill Brillhart."

"I'm beginning to realize how Archie feels."

"Yes. If he's right about what he claims."

"And he sounds oddly right."

"That's for you to decide," she said. "I have to fly."

We got a check.

Outside a cab came up and the doorman opened the door for her and helped her in. "I wish you were going to be along tonight at that," I said, and just at the last moment she turned, leaned over, and suddenly we kissed and I was left standing there with the pleasant taste of her lipstick on my mouth.

Another cab came and as I rode downtown I thought that so far it had started like a nice weekend.

# CHAPTER 4

## *The Island of St. John*

Despite fashionable New York's prejudice against being seen west of Fifth Avenue, Kira Winter lived in a terraced apartment on Central Park South close to Broadway. That at least is where she lived by herself; when she was home with her family, she also lived in apartments or houses on Beekman Place, at East Hampton and on Avenue Foch. She had taken the Central Park South apartment when she decided she wanted to be a popular singer instead of a poetess, which she had tried while still in finishing school, or a ceramist, which she had tried after the poetry, or a zither player, which she had tried after the ceramics. Everything considered, she was a rather intelligent girl and pleasant, lacking only one thing to be successful at something—the economic or social necessity for working hard at it.

So it was natural that, having decided to try getting into nightclub singing and the record business, like many another ambitious but less fortunate girl, she would move as close to Broadway as possible, and it was also natural that the place she moved into would be an enormous duplex apartment. If that makes her sound pretentious, I'm sorry, because she is not. She is a tall, wide, heavily boned girl, rather painfully aware I'd guess that she mostly resembles a good light heavyweight. It is a pity that her ambition should have settled on being a glamorous singer for, whatever her other qualities, none of the most expensive beauty salons in the world have ever been able to turn her broad, good-humored, plain face or indeterminately brown hair into anything but what they are.

Further, she is somewhat embarrassed by her family's money, and prefers the role of poor working girl to that of heiress. As a result she is often inclined, when she is in some third-rate joint, to throw her mink coat around carelessly and let it drag on the floor as though it were a wool markdown from Klein's basement, and some people take this for ostentation. It is really an effort at democracy. It never occurs to Kim that the first thing to do, if you really want to act as if your coat came from Klein's basement, is to go to Klein's basement and buy a coat there.

I learned most of this later. At the time I walked into her apartment I had never met her and I only knew her name vaguely as someone you read about in the columns. In a way, it didn't matter. I was doing all this mainly because Twit-Twit had a date that night and because I have a lot of curiosity. I didn't exactly believe that Brillhart was dead, but I didn't exactly believe he was alive. I didn't believe that anyone could have brought him back to life either, in spite of my medical researches of the past few days. I really did not believe, or disbelieve, anything, but my imagination was beginning to nag me. Because everyone in the whole case seemed believable.

The automatic elevator stopped at the twenty-fourth floor and I walked out into a noisy foyer.

Two other couples had arrived just ahead of me, one of them Eulalia and her brother. All of them were being greeted by a tall, heavy girl in a gold lame hostess suit that was undoubtedly chic but had not been made for someone like her. When the Popes caught sight of me I got a warm welcome and the gold lame girl, who was Kim Winter, said warmly she was glad I could come, which I thought was decent, considering how I'd let myself be forced on her. We went into the living room where there were two other couples and an extra man. I suddenly thought, this is Brillhart.

But the description didn't fit. He was dark and slender and had Broadway written all over him, from tasseled loafers to elaborately collared silk shirt. His name was Don Quayle, I learned, and he represented the music publisher who had published other Brillhart music and so was interested in the new score. The other couples were personal friends of Kim's, quiet, well-bred and strictly Beekman Place. It was an odd combination of people.

"Well, we're practically all here except for Brill," Kim said. "Coffee, anyone? You can't have anything to drink until you've heard the music. Nothing must interfere with that."

I looked around. It was a big, high-ceilinged, white-walled room which relatively little furniture made seem austere and barren. A stairway wound up from a corner of the room to the upper floor; beneath it was a sort of nook occupied by a concert grand piano. Ranged along the wall behind it was a row of photographs, inscribed to Kim. I recognized the faces of Porter, Rodgers, Loesser, Hammerstein, and several others. Along another wall were a dozen thin, beautifully formed Italian chairs and above them were two pictures, the only paintings in the room. One was a Picasso from his blue period and the other a Walt Kuhn clown. They weren't reproductions. It all was austere, and everything in it had cost a fortune.

The real feature was the window opposite—a wide, tall glass wall looking out on Central Park, before which were two enormous lounges, each the size of a double bed. The night was clear and the park glittered and gleamed and so did the huge rectangle of buildings surrounding it, and the stars in the dark sky above. Sky and land and lights stretched away; you felt you were seeing into infinity.

"Where *can* he be?" Eulalia said plaintively. "It's nine-thirty."

Quayle had carried his coffee cup to the piano. "Well, at least his manuscripts are here," he said. "I'd recognize those hen tracks anywhere. Look at *that,* for a lead sheet!"

"That isn't all of his that's here," Kim Winter drawled. "I had dinner with him a few nights ago. We came back here and I'm damned if he didn't leave his hat and raincoat."

"And I was supposed to take it and give it to him last night," said Eulalia. "Sorry, Kim."

"There it is," Kim said, gesturing. "I left it there by the door so he won't forget it tonight."

Quayle laughed. "That's funny. You know, I'll bet if you'll look in it you'll find a label from a store in New Haven, on Chapel Street. I was with him when he bought that coat, more than a dozen years ago. A show was opening up there and Brill was conducting the pit band. Lousy show, too. Closed after three consecutive performances."

"But where *is* he?" Eulalia was getting irritable. The Beekman Placers looked at her and kept to themselves.

"This is funny," Quayle said. He had been leafing through the music. "There are six songs here. Four of them I recognize. They're old things Brill tried to sell us years ago, and no dice. If he has sold these dogs to the movies he's sure some salesman. But the other two—Now this sounds rather nice. Listen."

His right hand, as he stood over the piano, rippled some notes.

"Stop it!" Kim demanded firmly. "Brill will be here any minute. He should introduce his own music—not you." She smiled and pouted simultaneously.

"Sorry," said Quayle. "How is he, anyway? I've not seen him much except for a glimpse day before yesterday as I was going by the Music Hall in a cab. He was in that old MG of his."

"That car," said Eulalia fondly.

"He looks tired," Kim said. "He told me he'd worked awfully hard on the Coast. In fact he's really beat. He looks like a man back from the grave."

We heard the elevator stop and we all turned toward the foyer. But the door did not open. Instead the arrival, who apparently did not know the layout, stayed in the elevator and beat a rhythmic knock on the apartment door. Brillhart?

"Well, at *last!* " said Kim and going into the foyer swung the door wide. But the man who stepped out was a slight, blond, hatless boy. "I hope I'm not late," he simpered. Kim introduced him; he too was a young singer.

While he made his entrance I edged over to the chair which held Brill-hart's hat and coat. It was an olive-drab trench coat, stained and worn and with a buckle missing from one of the sleeve straps. I wanted very much to see what was in the pockets. I bent over it, and a bell went off in my ear. It was the telephone in the foyer.

Kim said, "I gave my maid the night off. Would you mind picking that up, Mr. Deacon?"

I picked up the foyer telephone.

"Hello?"

"Hello." It was a husky man's voice. "Could I speak to Miss Winter?"

"I'll see if she's here," I said. "Should I tell her who's calling?"

"Yes," said the voice. "This is Brill Brillhart."

* * * *

I looked at the foyer wallpaper. It was black, with little white fawns leaping over it.

"Sorry. I didn't get the name."

"Brillhart," the voice repeated slowly. "Brill Brillhart. I'm supposed to be up there right now."

"Oh, sure. Just a moment."

I looked into the living room. Everyone was waiting. "It's Brillhart," I said and Kim came forward.

She said "Hello" into the phone. Then, "Darling, where the hell *are* you?" Then, "But, Brill, everybody's *here*... Well, how about in an hour?... But, Brill... Oh, all right." She began looking mad. "Oh, no, it's *perfectly* all right. Don will play it for us. We won't miss you at all." She hung up without saying good-by. "How do you like that!" she said and clicked indignantly into the living room.

"Mr. Brillhart is on the phone to the Coast," she said with bitter sarcasm. "They want changes in the lyrics and he and the writer are working them out via phone. It's going to take several hours. So we can twiddle our thumbs."

I did not follow her into the living room. One thing at a time is my motto. At the other side of the foyer was a door slightly ajar leading into a small powder-room lavatory. The only thing I could do was be bold and hope for the best. While they all watched Kim's golden bulk walk indignantly toward them as she made her announcement I picked up the raincoat and went into the lavatory. I locked the door. The pockets had a pipe, tobacco pouch, some well-worn pigskin gloves, and a letter. The letter was typed and had been air-mailed in Hollywood five days ago. It read:

Hi, Kid:

Everything's okay except one thing. They are thinking of dubbing some rhythm music with a patter lyric behind the island dance. I told them we could work it out on the phone between us. If they need it at all, it'll have to be done fast so stay close to your phone over the weekend, will you?

All the best and Eileen says hello.

—Al

P.S. Don't let them talk you into anything at the meeting Tuesday.

I looked in the tobacco pouch and smelled it; the tobacco was as dry as beach sand. The pipe was a Dunhill, well caked and with strong teethmarks in the bit. The gloves were for big hands, bigger than mine. The coat was dirty but it didn't *feel* worn. The label said it came from Abercrombie and Fitch. I made sure I remembered the date of the postmark on the otherwise-plain envelope and put everything back. But the pipe interested me. I used to smoke a pipe.

There was a bar of scented soap in the lavatory's chalice-like soap receptacle and it was not too hard. I soaked it a moment under the hot water tap and then made, as best I could, several impressions of the pipe's teethmarks in it. I wrapped the bar in Kleenex, put it in my pocket and told myself I was a damned fool.

I flushed the toilet for realism and went out. As I walked into the living room holding the coat behind me I dropped it on the chair and hoped nobody saw me. They were clustered around the piano where Quayle was opening the music. The soap bulged my pocket.

"I've got a date with him tomorrow night," Eulalia was saying to Kim. "And don't think I won't give him hell, honey." But she sounded smug.

"Have fun," said Kim.

"Date with Brillhart?" I asked Eulalia.

"Yes. He's picking me up in time for a little dinner, then we're catching that new pianist at the Embers. Brill says he does things way up on the keyboard that I should know about."

"She has a remarkably high range, you know, Mr. Deacon," said brother Frank, never a man to miss a trick.

"Let's get on with it," said Kim impatiently and I began to realize how things were between her and Eulalia. They both liked Brillhart—and Eulalia was a poor girl who was a working singer and Kim a rich girl but not a working singer.

Don Quayle sat down at the piano and looked at the sheaf of manuscript. "This first one is really just a rewrite of 'I'll Always Be Around,'" he said. "I remember telling Brill that a couple years ago when he first showed it to me."

"What's 'I'll Always Be Around?'" one of the Beekman Place women asked.

"'I'll always be around when you call,'" Eulalia trilled. "That was Brill's big hit. Of course he had several."

"I remember it," the woman—I think her name was Cookson—said politely. "Very pretty."

"When you hear this, you'll remember it again," said Quayle.

He ran through the song once, playing it with the simple, measured emphasis of the song plugger whose aim is only to fasten a melody in the hearer's memory. Then Eulalia sang it, in a capable but unmoving voice. There was applause from the Italian chairs where the others had taken seats and they ran through another song. Then Kim replaced Eulalia as soloist—I gathered it was like major league baseball, the visitors going to bat first—and we got two more. Kim sang a cool style, slow and purposefully a little flat. It didn't do the music any particular good, but I don't think anything could have done it much harm. All the songs sounded tired.

Apparently Quayle felt the same way. He turned the big sheet of musical manuscript over impatiently when he came to the end of the song, and said, "Brillhart may have missed his calling. Maybe he's a rock 'n' roll man at heart."

The other woman whose name I had not caught said, "You don't like rock 'n' roll?"

Quayle looked at her. He said, "Cutie, rock 'n' roll is, a guy takes off with a couple of shouts and records them on an assie. A publisher likes it, he's in business. That's music?"

Mrs. Cookson looked timid. "What's an assie?"

"An acetate record," said Kim. "It's a record made only to demonstrate a song to a publisher."

I said, "What's the name of this movie Brillhart composed for?"

Kim and Eulalia answered in unison: *"Caribbean Weekend."*

I said, "Those tunes don't have any particular Carib beat."

Quayle said, "You're right. Neither does this next one. But it's a nice song, and the lyric sort of fits into the idea."

He ran through it once and then played it a second time with expression and subtlety instead of emphasis, and he was right. This one had chords and harmony, and hearing it even for the first time you knew it was a song you were going to like and remember. It didn't sound like anything else.

Quayle swung into the chorus again, and Eulalia began to sing it. This time she sang with some color and feeling and the lyrics sounded good, too, and when it was finished the applause was genuine. The blond boy pouted. He hadn't been asked to sing.

"I gather the title is 'The Island of St. John,'" said Mrs. Cookson. "In the Virgins?"

"I would guess so. You've been there?"

There was a little conversation about the Virgin Islands, then he played the last song, which was nice but not what the previous one had been.

"Those last two make the score, if you ask me," said Quayle, getting up. "If anything will. We'd be interested in that St. John number."

Everyone looked around at everyone else. I suppose we all felt let down—by Brillhart's failure to appear, by the mostly unexciting music, and by the general feeling that it was Saturday night and too late to begin doing something else and too early to leave politely. Kim caught the feeling.

"Well, at least," she said, "we can have some wine. We were going to toast the composer, you know." She walked out and I followed her.

"Can I help, Miss Winter?"

"If you'd put some ice in an ice bucket it would help."

The kitchen contained every appliance ever advertised in a magazine. One of the two refrigerators contained a case of champagne. It was Moet '49. I filled two silver ice buckets while Kim got out a large bowl of caviar and some chopped egg. Nothing like a light snack, I thought. said, "Too bad about Brillhart. I'd like to have met him. I never have."

"You haven't missed much."

I laughed. "Don't be too mad. After all, he's probably up to his ears trying to turn out that song. And musicians are always unreliable."

"That musician certainly is. He is my voice coach, and I pay him a very fair fee, I can assure you. But I never know whether I'm going to get a lesson or just an alibi on the phone."

"He sounds like a sort of will-o'-the-wisp."

"Oh, he's far from that when he wants to be. He can be around plenty when he feels like it." Again I caught the woman-scorned intonation. "I'll tell you what he's really like. You've heard the joke about the first psychiatrist who ever got to heaven?"

"I don't think I have."

"It defines Brill perfectly. There was this psychiatrist who died and went to heaven and when St. Peter stopped him at the Pearly Gates and asked him who he was he explained he was a psychiatrist. 'What's that?' says St. Peter. 'We've never had a psychiatrist up here. You must be the first.' So the psychiatrist explained that he treated people for various mental disturbances and hallucinations and the like, and St. Peter said, 'You have cured people of hallucinations?' and the psychiatrist said, 'Sure, often.' Would you hand me that silver tray?"

I handed it to her.

"So St. Peter said, 'Come right in, friend, we can use you. I'll take you to your first patient right now.' So he and the psychiatrist walked down the street and came across a guy walking around with his nose in the air, looking very proud of himself and very contemptuous of everyone else, and St. Peter says, 'There's your man.' And the psychiatrist says, 'Oh, yes. Delusions of grandeur, obviously. Who is he?' And St. Peter says, 'Well, I'll tell you who he is. That's God Almighty—but he thinks that he is Brill Brillhart, the voice coach.'"

I laughed. "Is Brillhart really that bad?"

"You saw what he did tonight. And how late he called. He could have dropped in for half an hour anyway. He has no respect for anyone except himself. Can you carry both buckets?"

"Sure."

We drank the cold wine out of big glasses and helped ourselves to caviar and talked in a subdued, make conversation way. I am not fond of champagne and I put my glass down as soon as I could and went over to the piano and studied the hen-track musical notation on the manuscripts. I've seen lead sheets before and Brillhart's were unusually illegible. I looked at the pictures above the piano and the names scrawled on them. One read "Fond love and admiration for Kim—Brill Brillhart."

I found myself studying a good-looking, slightly beefy face with a lot of curly hair and a wide, infectious smile that was just a little too self-confident. It was my first look at Brillhart.

I left soon after. A little fast footwork at the door enabled me to dodge Frank Pope. I thanked Kim and she thanked me for coming and we both meant it.

Outside it was cold and clear and just turned eleven, the time and the kind of night that make you want to do something. And I knew what I wanted to do; the ideas were beginning to come. But first I walked toward Fifth, thinking over what I had seen and heard, and about the bar of soap in my pocket, and passing the Plaza I suddenly knew that Archie Sinclair was right and that Brillhart was dead.

I stopped in a drugstore and called Archie but there was no answer. While I waited, listening to the bell ring, the rhythm of the rings and of the song merged in my mind and I began humming Brillhart's one good tune.

I walked to his apartment and let myself into the foyer with the passkey. I wondered if the caretaker had yet tried to use the key I'd left. I also wondered if he was around. I went up in the elevator and let myself into Brillhart's apartment.

I switched on a light, looked at the silent piano and then, walking softly, went over to a desk where there was a pipe rack. I took several of the pipes and looked at the bits. The teethmarks looked the same. I took the soap out of my pocket and fitted one of the bits, as best I could, against the little tooth-like projections from the soap. It was anything but scientific, but as nearly as I could tell, they fitted. So it was a genuine Brillhart pipe in the coat pocket. But was it Brillhart's coat? I looked through the few closets. There was no other raincoat of any sort hanging in any of them.

I sat down on the living-room sofa and looked around. In front of me there was a coffee table and on it was a cup and saucer. The cup contained a few spoonfuls of black coffee. I smelled it; it smelled fresh. I might be wrong, but I was fairly sure it had not been there when I was in the room earlier.

I got up, took off my coat and hat, and switched out all the lights. As I did, the phone began to ring. It rang a long time, a ghostly sound in the empty apartment, while I debated answering it. Finally I snapped the light on again, put a finger between my teeth to change my articulation, and said "Hello" into the phone.

A man said, "Brill?"

"Who's calling?"

"Is this Brill Brillhart?"

"Who is calling?" I demanded, trying to sound tough and drunk.

"I guess I've got the wrong number," he said and hung up.

I waited but he did not call back. So I switched out the lights and sat down.

I sat there for an hour and a half. But nobody came and nothing happened, except that someone in the building not too far away was having a party and it sounded like a good one.

* * * *

At 1 a.m. I turned the lights on again and dialed Archie Sinclair.

Archie's voice said, "Hello?" huskily.

"Did I wake you up?"

"No. I just got in."

"Archie, I've been working on your little problem and I'm beginning to see some light. I want to talk to you. Now."

He was silent.

I said, "Are you with someone?"

"No. But..."

"Then I'm coming over and you are going to tell me what you know about this guy's death."

"Deac, I can't do that. Really. Look, I just came back from the hospital and I've got to go back."

"You're sick?"

"*I'm* not. No."

"Then who is?"

He was silent again. Then he asked. "Where are you?"

"Midtown." There was no point in telling him more than he would tell me. "I can come to your place."

"It'll take you forever. I'm in Riverdale. But I've got an idea. Want to go for a ride?"

"Only if you will tell me what I want to know."

"Well." He was either reluctant or calculating. "Okay. Where'll I pick you up? I'll be in the car."

"Make it Reuben's on Fifty-eighth—you know? I want to get a sandwich."

"I'll be in front at a quarter of two."

"Make it two o'clock. I hate to gulp."

"Good enough. And—thanks for calling. I appreciate it even if it doesn't seem that way."

I switched out the light, made sure the apartment door was locked, and went down in the elevator without meeting anyone.

Being a burglar is not necessarily as complicated as people make out.

# CHAPTER 5

## *The Watches of the Night*

When I came out of Reuben's, the February night smelled late and cold and exciting. Cabs were speeding through Fifty-eighth Street, taking people to places they probably shouldn't be going, but were in a hurry to get to, and would have fun at. I'd like to be doing that, I thought, and for a moment I wished I had not mixed myself up in this. But at the curb Archie was hunched over the wheel of a black Jaguar 3.4.

I said, "Sorry to be late. I'm an army that travels on its stomach."

"I just pulled up. You don't mind a ride?"

"Not if you're going to talk."

"The Doctors' and Nurses' Clinic is where we're going, near Syosset, out on the Island. Ever hear of it?"

"No. That's the hospital you referred to on the phone?"

"Yes."

"Something urgent?"

"Urgent."

He wheeled down to Fifty-seventh, heading for the Queensboro bridge. When we were on it, I said, "Suppose you spin the tale."

"Not now, if you don't mind." He was apologetic. "I did some thinking driving downtown. I decided the only thing for me to do is to tell you every-thing, and trust in your—your discretion. I'm going to do that. But I don't want to try to tell it while I'm driving. It means too much. There'll be time at the hospital."

Okay, but it had better be good, I thought. "I'll shut up while you drive."

"Oh, talking won't bother me. In fact I'm curious to learn what you've found out."

Sure, I thought. I'm supposed to tell everything. I wondered how much I should tell. I said, "Well, for one thing, I think you're right. I've a hunch your friend Brillhart is dead."

Archie laughed. "That isn't news. I told you that long ago."

"And I heard you. On the other hand, I also heard Brillhart. Tonight. On the phone. I talked to him."

I waited for the explosion, but it didn't come. His lips tightened as he watched the lights of Northern Boulevard spin past.

I went on. "Tonight I saw the coat Brillhart left at a girl's house a night or two back. In it was a letter he had received from a friend in Hollywood, written only a few days before. There was one of his pipes in the coat and I can assure you it was really Brillhart's pipe. I checked. Oddly enough, I tend to believe you, Archie, for reasons I don't want to go into at the moment. But I can tell you that there are a hell of a lot of people in the world who think Brillhart's very much alive, and say they have seen him, and have eaten with him, and talked to him, and I suspect have been kissed by him. So whenever we get to the hospital and you feel like telling your side of the story, I'll listen with considerable interest. That's about all I'll tell you right now."

He didn't say anything, and I a little wished I hadn't said it. But it was time he was jarred into something.

We drove through Manhasset in silence.

* * * *

The Doctors' and Nurses' Clinic was a sprawling two-story brick building set back from a side road a mile or so from the parkway. Only the letters D.N.C. on a white light globe over the door identified it. When Archie rang the night bell a nurse admitted us with an emotionless, "Good evening." Apparently he was known; he led the way to an elevator and we got off at the second floor.

Halfway down a dark, medicine-scented corridor a nurse sat in the glow of the night desk, the scratch of her pen audible from thirty feet away in that quiet. She looked up.

"Oh, Mr. Sinclair." She was young and rather cute. "I'm so sorry we called you." She batted her eyes to show her regret. "Because now it seems everything is all right. Dr. Valda is with him and will be for a while. But it appears that it was just one of those flurries. You know—he's had them before."

"Sure. Don't worry about calling me. It was what I asked you to do. He—he hardly has anyone else. Will you tell Dr. Valda we'll be in the waiting room, when he's finished?"

"Of course, Mr. Sinclair." She smiled.

The waiting room was small and furnished in the chintz-and flower-print style with which hospitals try to cheer up their visitors without being too conspicuously hilarious. We took off our coats, pulled up chairs and Archie closed the door and drew out cigarettes. The waiting room was stuffy and I opened a window a little. From far away came the hum of a late car. Otherwise it was country-quiet and country-dark.

"They seem to know you."

"I've been out to see him regularly for the past two or three weeks. He's going steadily downhill. Rotten, isn't it?"

"Sure. But don't bother to tell me who he is. Let's just play Twenty Questions."

Archie leaned back against the chair, closed his eyes and breathed out cigarette smoke. "I'm going to tell you," he said. "Now. There'll be time—Valda is very thorough. He's not the regular doctor on this case. He's my own—my psychiatrist, in fact. And when I tell you, you'll realize how much this really is not my secret at all and never has been. And how frightening and crazy the whole thing is. And why each time I run across these traces of Brillhart—This is no way to begin."

"That's true."

He pulled deeply on the cigarette and then began speaking in a low, deliberate voice, pausing occasionally to consider his words, like a man anxious to get everything exactly right, and neither to understate nor to overstate.

"The man down the corridor, whom I've been referring to and who is dying of a heart ailment, is Rudolf Jersey. He is sixty-eight years old, and I suppose he is the best friend I've had in all my life. You know who he is, of course."

"The song writer and composer."

Archie smiled gently. "I'm glad you added 'composer.' That is what he basically is. It's true that he has written a lot of popular songs. All his music has always been popular. But after he got into the theater and could compose for a more sophisticated audience he wrote what I think is really fine music. And some of his serious things, which he will never allow to be published in his lifetime but which he used to play for us at times—well, this is a great man, Deac. Or was.

"He came to this country when he was sixteen years old, a cabin boy on a Polish freighter sailing out of Gdynia. The original name was Jerczey, of course. He jumped ship, starved, washed dishes, slept in Bowery doorways, and finally got a job playing piano in a beer garden. As soon as he learned the language he began writing songs and trying to sell them. That's the early part. You know the later one. By the time he was thirty he was famous and rich—the ASCAP list of his hits is as long as your arm.

"When he was thirty-five Rudolf met a French singer named Hortense de Clerque. Hortense had been brought over here for a show by some producer who'd heard her sing in Paris, where she was very big. In New York she wasn't. Rudolf wrote the score for the show and it was a hit but the critics didn't like Hortense. She was crushed and Rudolf felt sorry for her. Judging from her pictures, she was one of those fragile, Piaf-like things, all dark sad eyes and pathos and helplessness.

"Well, that was it. Rudolf, the Polish immigrant who never noticed women, and Hortense, the sad little French failure, fell in love. They were married. It was a happy marriage while it lasted. They had a child a couple years later, also christened Hortense, who became la petite Hortense in the family. Then, when la petite Hortense was four, her mother was killed in an auto crash up in Rockland County, where they'd taken a house for the summer.

"Maybe you can guess what this did to Rudolf. He devoted himself to the little Hortense, immersed himself more and more in music, and paid less and less attention to the rest of the world. He began doing considerably more serious composition, incidentally, but if you study it you will see that all his music took on a somber tone. Even his popular stuff shows up with melancholy twists and minor key releases, if you know what I mean.

"In case you wonder how I know all of this, it's because Rudolf told me. He and I became friends about eight years ago. I had come back to New York from Paris, determined to do something musically, and I was invited to a cocktail party and Rudolf was there. I talked to him for almost fifteen minutes, because I was a stranger and knew almost no one at the party, and he seemed to be in the same situation. I told him what I hoped to do musically. Later I asked someone who the old guy was. When they told me, I felt like slinking out. I'd been telling Rudolf Jersey what I hoped to do in music—the guy who had already done everything! Yet he had been sympathetic and even asked me to call him sometime."

Out on the parkway a police siren wailed up to its high and slowly died. It made me feel the darkness outside, and think of how many people inside might be lying, eyes open, waiting for day to break and for hope to come back.

"I didn't dream of calling him," Archie said. "But he called me. He asked me to come around sometime. Well, I did. He lived in this slightly colossal town house in the East Sixties—terribly handsome and expensive. And lonesome."

Archie lit another cigarette and thought a moment.

"What had happened was that after his wife died he'd put his whole life into little Hortense. Then, when she was twenty, she died. Actually, she had killed herself. At twenty! The night that I had met him had been the first time he had gone out since then. That was the beginning of a real friendship, although he contributed everything to it, advising me and criticizing my efforts at music, and I contributed nothing."

I said, "I expect you're being too modest. Jersey recognized your ability and enjoyed your company."

"Hell with that." He crushed out the cigarette, then reached for his pack. "I'll come to the point. Hortense's death did something to Rudolf. He closed up her bedroom in the house, for instance, and never let anyone go in there—anyone. He went there himself, though. He told me he used to go in there and pray."

There was a knock at the door. The night nurse put her head in. "I'm going down for coffee, Mr. Sinclair. Could I bring you gentlemen some?"

We said she could and she closed the door and Archie said, "Here's the point. Rudolf has had this heart condition for years. Last year his doctor said he should get out of the town house, where he had to walk up so many stairs, or else install an elevator. That couldn't be done, architecturally speaking, without tearing down half the house. So Rudolf decided to move. That meant dismantling his daughter's room.

"Six months ago he began going through drawers and closets that had not been touched for years. That's when he found it."

He fell silent; then—"There's one little thing I haven't mentioned. Remember the show, *Look to the Future,* years ago? Rudolf wrote the music for it. And Brill Brillhart wrote the lyrics. They stank."

"You don't like Brillhart?"

"Let's skip that for now. The thing is, Rudy and Brill were naturally close at this point. And little Hortense sort of went for Brill. Naturally Brill was at the Jersey house a lot while they were writing the show, and he and Hortense got friendly and then the show opened and flopped. Some months later Hortense killed herself."

"I gather there was a connection."

"There was."

"I can guess."

"Sure. Hortense had really fallen for Brillhart. And Brillhart—well—was Brillhart. After a while she got the idea she was pregnant. Marriage wasn't in Brillhart's plans; for one thing, he was already married. For another, the show flopped and he knew he was washed up as far as Rudolf was concerned. Too many *good* lyricists around. Brillhart bowed out. He's good at that. He knows when.

"And Hortense, lonely and frightened, with no one she could confide in, killed herself. Sleeping pills. At the time, no one knew why."

"They usually perform autopsies on suicides," I said.

"They did on this one. She wasn't pregnant. In a way, she had been doubly betrayed."

"I see. How did your friend Rudolf find out?"

"From her diary and some notes from Brillhart he found under her lingerie in a drawer, when they had to dismantle that untouched bedroom. Remember, this was just six months ago. Rudolf almost went crazy."

Efficient heels started down the hall.

"Maybe he did go crazy," Archie said. "He brooded on it for a while, I know. It was back in December when he decided on what he was going to do. He was old and sick, and wouldn't live long. He had no one left who mattered, and there was this man who had taken from him the one thing in his world that was precious to him."

The waiting room door opened and the nurse hurried in, looking cheerful and holding two cups of coffee. "I hope these didn't get cold." She left.

I doubt if Archie heard her. He was frowning across the room.

"Rudolf decided to kill Brillhart," he said. "And that's what he did. Very easily. Two months ago."

# CHAPTER 6

## *How Brillhart Went Out*

It was good coffee.

"Rudolf planned it all carefully," Archie said, sipping it. "He would kill Brillhart in cold blood, luring him into a trap, then telling him what he was going to do and why. Afterward he would calmly announce to the world what he had done, admit his guilt, but also reveal Brillhart for what he was. What might happen to Rudolf thereafter would not matter—he hadn't long to live, anyway.

"When he had everything planned, Rudolf called Brillhart, whom he hadn't seen in years, and invited him up to his apartment. He told Brillhart he wanted to discuss a new score and naturally Brillhart bit."

"Why naturally?"

"Rudolf was still a big name to be associated with and the girl was long dead—you don't think the *ethical* side of it would occur to Brillhart?"

I thought about this a little. "Archie, you seem to have a lot against Brillhart. Is it all really because of your friend Rudolf and his daughter?"

Archie's face tightened and the long sallow nose became the color of a white candle. "No. I'll tell you, if you want to know. Last fall I went to a party at the Waldorf. It was given by Cole Porter to introduce his score for a new show to the record companies; a guy I know with RCA-Victor asked me along. Brillhart was there—he was A and R man for some small label at the time. He got pretty drunk and began abusing me. Why, I don't know, for we'd never even seen each other. But that was my introduction to Brillhart. Finally I got mad and talked back and he hit me. Twice. I'm not much of a fighter. I went down.

"When I came to, a nice girl named Mary Newton was putting cold cloths on my face and apologizing for Brillhart. That's how I met Mary."

"So?"

"So now you know why I don't like Brillhart. I don't think it's just because he hit me. I think it's because he made me feel inept and ridiculous before someone I have since come to like. Mary and I gradually became friendly. A week ago, we became engaged."

"I see."

"But two months before, Rudolf had invited Brillhart to his apartment, which is in one of the big new buildings near River House. He had sent his man out for the evening, so he himself led Brillhart into the library, patting him on the back. Then, when Brillhart was comfortable and looking happy, Rudolf took out a thirty-eight pistol—he had a second in his dressing-gown pocket but he never needed it—and told Brillhart what he knew and what he planned to do."

"I gather Rudolf told you all this?"

"Yes. Brillhart panicked and started to get up. Rudolf shot him in the right shoulder—he'd even thought the shots out in advance. He didn't want to kill him too quickly. That first shot not only slowed Brillhart down, but it also convinced him. I must say, I sort of admire Rudolf here. A man of sixty-eight, taking the law into his own hands and knowing what the consequences would be.

"For his plan was simple. He was going to explain to Brillhart the enormity of his crime and that he was about to die for it. Then, when everything was clear, it was Rudolf's idea to start shooting. When Brillhart was dead, he would wait for the people who would hear the shots to come charging in. Then he was going to tell them what he had done, and why, and take the punishment.

"Well, he did everything just as he had planned. And it worked. When Brillhart heard what he was up against he tried to get out of his chair once more and Rudolf fired again, and after that Brillhart crouched in his chair, watching the gun, a big, shaking animal. When Rudolf had said what else he had to say, he began firing carefully. He said he laughed as he did it. I suppose he did. Then he sat back and waited. But something went wrong."

"He didn't hit hint?"

Archie smiled wearily. "He hit him all right. Plenty. No, what went wrong was something else. There was a knock at the door almost immediately. Rudolf answered it. It was the woman in the duplex across the foyer with whom he was slightly acquainted. She apologized for bothering him but she and her husband had been playing some records and had got into an argument—which Beethoven quartet was it that contains a Russian song? She knew Rudolf would know instantly."

Archie smiled at the irony. "She had heard nothing, and she occupied the only other apartment on that floor. Rudolf told her it was the Seventh and she left. Then he went back to the library.

"He sat there for perhaps half an hour. Brillhart was slouched in the chair, blood staining his shirt front. But nothing else happened. No one had heard anything."

I said, "That's no miracle. The walls in any decently built apartment could muffle the sound of a thirty-eight. Especially if the nearest people were playing records."

"Exactly. Anyway, after thirty or forty minutes, Rudolf began to get an entirely different idea. Maybe he could win a more complete revenge. Maybe he could not only kill Brillhart but get away with it. He has told me since that what attracted him was not any real desire to escape, but rather the idea of stamping out Brillhart as though he were a poisonous insect, without penalty—the supreme insult. Besides, Brillhart had died thinking Rudolf's shots would be heard and he'd at least be caught and punished. To outwit Brillhart on this too would be an even more perfect revenge.

"I said Rudolf lives in one of the new apartment buildings. It has a garage in the basement, and he has a car. And he has one of those collapsible chromium wheel chairs, going back to his heart attacks. He examined the body. There was a little blood on the back of the chair where Brillhart had been sitting, but not much—his clothing had absorbed it—and the bullet holes were hardly noticeable in the tapestry upholstery.

"You get the idea now. He loaded the body into the wheel chair, boldly took it down in the garage elevator, which is self-service, and hoped for the best. I know it sounds crazy but actually the gamble wasn't so great. It was fairly late and, as Rudolf figured it, if anyone else rang to stop the elevator he could hold the door shut and push the button again. And of course in a way he didn't really give a damn. Supposing he was caught—he'd never figured to get away with it anyway.

"There's only one guy on duty in the garage at night and Rudolf's car stall is near the elevator. He had no trouble in trundling the body over to his Cadillac without being seen, and dumping it into the back seat. The chair he folded up and put in the trunk. Then he drove out. He had committed the perfect crime—by accident.

"It was getting on toward midnight and he didn't know where to go with a body. For a time he thought of the rivers, and using the chair as a weight. He even thought of just driving to a police station and giving himself up.

"But he'd spent a number of weekends up in the Rockland County area. He remembered it as wild and mountainous. And that is where his wife had died."

"Poetic justice."

"Exactly. He began driving, not caring much what happened. When he told me about it later that night he wasn't even sure whether he went across George Washington or the Tappan Zee bridge. Anyway he kept going, up

9-W and then after a while back into the hills and then the mountains and off the main roads onto the side ones, then the lesser side ones and then onto gravel trails. Finally, when he felt he had climbed far into the blackest hills there are over there, he dragged the body out and hauled it across a field and into woods and finally left it. But only after taking the wallet and wrist watch that Brillhart had, so he could not be identified. Going back, he almost got lost."

"Did he cut the labels out of Brillhart's clothes?"

"The labels? I don't think so."

"How about the laundry marks on his linen—shirts and so on?"

"I—I don't suppose Brillhart had any laundry marks on his clothes."

"Everyone does—unless he does his own laundry."

Archie looked alarmed.

"I don't know. All I know is he had a hell of a time finding his way back to the car. Oh, one other thing he took was a flask Brillhart had in his jacket, because it was initialed. Two bullets had punctured it. When he got back to the car he discovered he still had Brillhart's Alpine hat and old green trench coat."

"I know. With a label saying it had been bought from a men's store on Chapel Street in New Haven."

Even though I'd a little anticipated it, the way he jumped up startled me. But, I suppose, not as much as I had startled him.

"You..." he said wildly. "How the hell do you know that?"

It was a good thing he had drunk the coffee. The cup rattled in its saucer.

"How do *you* happen to know it?"

"I burned the coat, that's why. I suppose you knew that too?"

"No. Tell me about it."

But his face was still fearful. "How did you know where that coat came from?"

"I'll explain. Relax. You're doing the talking now. Finish it up."

"There's not much more. Rudolf found the car at last. It was daylight by the time he got back on 9-W. It was a little after eight when he showed up at my place."

"Your place?"

"I told you he sort of looked on me as a son. I live up in Riverdale. In an apartment overlooking Spuyten Duyvil."

"So I gather."

"Sorry. I'm not tracking tonight. Anyway, Rudolf showed up a little after eight that morning. He woke me up. He still had the coat and flask and hat. And he was on the very edge of collapse. I gave him some coffee and tried to make him lie down but he had to tell me everything, and he did. Sometimes he laughed as he told the story, and once he wept. Finally I got some sleeping pills into him and lifted him into my bed. He slept until seven that night. Then we took care of the details. I burned the coat and wallet in the fireplace and threw the watch into the river late that night. The flask would have gone the same way but I'd begun feeling guilty about the whole thing, and I got an irrational idea that someone might see the gleam as I tossed it into the water. So I kept it. In fact I still have it."

"I'd like to see it."

"You can."

"And so?"

"That's all. When Rudolf woke up that evening I took him home and saw that he got into bed. I had his doctor come over and told a lie about his rehearsing all night. The doctor gave him a sedative and I stayed with him. Next day we didn't talk about it; we waited for repercussions."

"But they didn't come. There was no news. That was two months ago, and there hasn't been any news since."

"None at all?"

"Oh, sure. But not immediately."

"What do you mean?"

"Rudolf had taken the body so far up into the foothills, if you know that country—well, it was only a few days ago that the body was discovered."

"Brillhart's *body?*"

"Of course. I have a clipping from the *Herald Tribune* I'll show you."

"You mean the body's been identified?"

"Of course not! Not yet. But it was Brillhart's body, all right. I'll show you."

"I see."

"You understand, don't you, why I wasn't anxious to tell you all this earlier? I mean, Rudolf is dying. Once he's gone, it won't matter. But you see why I *know* Brillhart's dead."

"Then how do you account for his being around?"

"Because somebody knows something. Or maybe it's just guilt."

"It can't be just guilt. And yet..."

"Yet what?" Archie said.

"Who could, as you say, know something? Where are the vulnerable areas? Supposing, for instance, someone knew Brillhart was going up to see Rudolf that night—Brillhart seems to have been the kind who might have boasted about it in a name-dropping way. But if so, why hasn't the person who knew raised a clamor? Then there's the chance, in spite of what you say, that someone saw him leave the apartment with the body. Or saw and recognized him out in the darkest reaches of Rockland County. Either seems hardly possible. Still..."

"I told you the whole thing is insane."

"It isn't insane—yet. There are at least two other possibilities. One is that Rudolf himself talked. Since he told you about it, why not someone else?"

"Impossible! He told me in an extremity of exhaustion. But he is too intelligent and too thoughtful to burden his friends with guilty secrets, in ordinary circumstances. What's your other possibility?"

I didn't want to go into it. "Just a fanciful idea, born of a story I've been working on. There's what medical researchers call resuscitation—the bringing the dead back to life, under certain optimum circumstances. But I don't think they could have existed here."

Archie looked at me suspiciously. "You're kidding?"

"No. But I might as well be. For if it had happened, why would Brillhart not come forward and prosecute the man who attempted to kill him? Maybe he couldn't charge him with murder, as long as he himself was alive. But there's always felonious assault, or attempted murder. And he could sure sue for damages!"

"And Brillhart's the type to."

"Sure. One other thing. Did lots of people see the fight between you and Brillhart that night at the party?"

"Sure," said Archie moodily. "If you'd call it a fight. And that reminds me. I guess you had better know everything."

The nurse's white-capped head with black velvet bow appeared in the door. "Dr. Valda would like a word with Mr. Sinclair."

"Thanks. I've got to talk to Valda."

"Not before you tell me what you were about to say."

"It's not so important." He looked around to make sure the nurse's head had withdrawn. "Well—Mary Newton and I are—are shacked up. She's the first girl I've really loved—you know what I mean. We're getting married, of course."

"Don't be so defensive."

"I didn't mean to be. But it was a good thing she was out tonight when you called."

"She doesn't know about Brillhart?"

Archie laughed, not humorously. "Mary B. Newton doesn't know!"

"I guess I should get something out of that."

"The B is for Brillhart. She's Mary Brillhart Newton—his sister. She's the girl who took care of me the night Brillhart slugged me. He'd brought her to the party. I didn't learn who she really was until I had taken her out several times. She was ashamed of her brother and what he had done, and I guess she liked me. And there was the different name, of course. She'd married this guy Newton, who was a BOAC pilot, and divorced him three years ago."

"And now you're engaged." I digested that.

"That's right. We've—we've been living together. How can I tell her what I know about her brother's murder? Or that I'm an accessory to it, in a way?"

"Were she and her brother very close? They sound so different."

"Not really close. They had gone their own ways for years. Mary was a nurse, then an airline stewardess. That's how she met Newton; they lived in Singapore, mostly. But she is a warm-hearted girl, and she and her brother have no other kin in the world. I think her feeling toward him is the warmth born of loneliness."

The *warmth of loneliness* was rather eloquent, I thought, and explained a lot about both her and Archie. I was about to say something when a thin little man with a mustache and a big head of hair came in. He said, "Achille," pronouncing it correctly, "good evening."

Archie introduced us. "Mind if we leave you a minute, Deac?"

"You stay and I'll go. I feel like stretching my legs."

I ambled down to the end of the corridor and stood looking out the window into the darkness. Behind me the nurse scribbled. Far off I could see the parkway, with lights of cars moving across it like luminous beads sliding infrequently along a wire.

When Archie called me, I knew what I was going to do.

"Dr. Valda has made a careful examination and finds no cause for alarm," he said. His face looked peaceful.

"That is not quite what I said," the doctor corrected him. "There *is* cause for alarm, I am sorry to say. But there are no immediate indications of—of trouble. You realize that a man of sixty-eight, with an advanced coronary, can run into serious difficulty at any time. Witness the attack earlier today. But at the moment I think we can relax."

"I'd like to ask a favor," I said. "As I understand it, Dr. Valda has just made an examination of Mr. Jersey, but he is not Mr. Jersey's regular doctor. He is yours, Archie. Right?"

Archie's expression tightened. "He is my psychiatrist. He has been treating me for upwards of two years." Dr. Valda nodded agreement. He seemed tirelessly cheerful, even at 3 a.m. "I asked him to come out at this time of night because—well, I do not think too much of Rudolf's regular doctor."

"All right. I want to talk to your doctor alone for a few minutes. You've asked my help—in a certain matter. I want your permission to ask Dr. Valda some questions about you. In private."

Archie blinked, but he said, "Okay. Tell him anything he wants to know, doctor," and went outside.

I hoped he didn't think I was too much of a heel.

When we were alone, I shook my head at Valda's silver cigarette case. He said, "Regardless of what permissions my patient might give, Mr. Deacon, you understand there are only a limited number of things I can tell you." He squinted good-humoredly, not a young man, the bushy hair and mustache suspiciously black.

"I realize. On the other hand, I am investigating a matter that may concern your patient's sanity and certainly his future well-being. If what I ask is unethical—well, I hope it won't be, for I need the answers. I hope you'll remember that in deciding what is ethical and what isn't. I have ethics too."

"You are frank. Good."

"Good. First, about Mr. Jersey. You've never seen him before?"

"Not professionally. I have met him, a couple of times, with Mr. Sinclair."

"You're a psychiatrist. Did you get any impression of emotional disturbance?"

Puzzlement made his face flicker. "No."

"I mean, melancholia? Morbid anxiety? Hallucinations, delusions, or anything like that—you know what I mean. I don't know the jargon."

"No. I know what you mean. But no."

"Then"—I took a breath—"in your opinion Mr. Jersey could not have gotten a mistaken idea that he had, ah, committed a terrible crime, for example?"

"Without having done it?"

"That's what I mean."

Dr. Valda smiled. "No."

I said, "We come to Mr. Sinclair. You've been treating him. I don't know what for. I don't care. But do you think he is subject to any sort of disturbance that might make him exaggerate things to himself, or get involved in elaborate fantasies, or—well, I told you I don't know the language."

Dr. Valda smiled again. More pleasantly.

"Mr. Deacon, let me tell you something. So many people are becoming so worried about themselves and so knowledgeable about psychiatry these days that we psychiatrists have trouble directing ourselves to those who really need help. That is the case here. Mr. Jersey has a bad heart. That is a physical ailment that no one can cure. Mr. Sinclair has some maladjustments, as do most people, and like most people he could work them out without professional help. I have told him this, I assure you. But he does like to come to me. I think he won't much longer. He is getting married, as I am sure you know. I think his wife-to-be, who is a very wonderful woman, will do a lot for him. So...well, there is nothing more I can say, Mr. Deacon. Neither of these people has any real emotional disturbance. That is what I think you wanted to know. Now—I confirm it. So. I will be getting on. So nice to meet you."

The black hair shook sincerely over our handclasp.

# CHAPTER 7

*Ghost Music*

While the Jaguar hummed toward town Archie said, "I forgot. I mentioned a clipping."

Driving with one hand he shook little papers out of his wallet and handed me one. It was a news clipping from the *Herald Tribune*.

### MAN'S CORPSE FOUND IN ROCKLAND COUNTY

Haverstraw, February 23—The body of a man about 40, partly decomposed and with all valuables removed, was found in a patch of woods today by surveyors for the new throughway exit.

Preliminary examination indicated he had been shot, probably several times. State police said the man's shoes indicated he had been dragged a considerable distance.

I handed it back. "Interesting. But not conclusive. The time checks, though."

"And the shots."

"Yes."

"One other thing. Here."

I took another slip from him and looked at it. It was a check for $2,500. It was made out to me.

I said, "Oh, hell."

"No hells, Deac. It's for expenses and all that. This thing isn't over."

"I think it is."

"What do you mean?"

I didn't want to answer. It was all obvious, I was tired, and most of all, I was irritated by Archie's helplessness and way with money. Brillhart was dead, and the rest would presently be explained. What remained was just a mopping up.

But there was no point in starting anything at this time of night. "Oh, nothing." I closed my eyes. The check I put in my pocket, to give back later.

The Jaguar hummed.

When I opened my eyes again, a sign said, *Whitestone Bridge Bear Right.*

"What do you mean, you think it's over?"

"Let me explain later." I added a lie. "I want to think a little more about the whole God-damned thing."

He nodded agreement, but he also added gently, "You shouldn't swear like that, you know," and took me back to my uncle's truck garage and a certain Irish truck driver. I closed my eyes, smiling.

After a little he began whistling a tune under his breath. I'd heard the song a few hours before, at Kim's. It was the Virgin Islands song, "The Island of St. John." I listened until there was no doubt about it.

"That's pretty. Something you wrote?"

"Gosh, no." He turned, pleased. "I'm not that good. That is Rudolf's. One of the songs he left in manuscript and would never allow to be published. No one knows that melody except me. Perhaps little Hortense heard it."

"I see."

* * * *

When I got home I got into pajamas and opened a can of beer. For half an hour I sat listening to an all-night radio program, sipping beer, and ignoring Brillhart. Then I went to bed and slept like a log.

For three hours. Then there was a weather change.

I was awakened by a window shade snapping loudly twice, and then rustling against itself, a slow, slithering sound. Wind that was cold and fresh as an ocean gale was pouring through the apartment.

I had been deeply asleep and probably dreaming. I must have been.

For Brillhart was at the foot of my bed, hunched over low, leaning toward me, staring.

I could see the silhouette of his hat and the bulky shoulders in the trench coat. It seemed as though I could make out his unblinking eyes.

For a moment I lay rigid in panic.

Then I came out of my drowse, and realized I was staring wide-eyed at my own hat and coat draped over a ladder-back chair at the foot of the bed, where I'd thrown them when I came in.

I hated myself, and laughed and cursed my stupidity out loud in simultaneous relief and disgust.

In a little while I got back to sleep, but before I did I thought a bit about the strange immortality of a man who was dead and yet continued to affect other people's lives.

Like mine.

# CHAPTER 8

## *A Gathering of Friends*

When I picked up Twit-Twit a few hours later it was raining like hell. I was still tired. I said, "I hate your dress," and Twit-Twit said, "You're too stupid to appreciate Ann Fogarty," and I said, "I hope you had a lousy time last night, because I did."

Twit-Twit said, "I wound up at the Stork again, and I'll bet you bribed the bastard I was with to take me there, you son of a bitch."

I began to cheer up.

Twit-Twit can stay up all night and still look good, and the dress wasn't really bad. I said, "You can walk," because the Dolans live only a half block from her place and I had an umbrella, and sometimes I like rain. So we walked close together through the rain, which was heavy but cold and refreshing, and it was nice to feel my arm around her and to know she liked it there.

The Dolans' apartment is not large and you might think it rather scrubby, until you learn that the antique pistols and old playbills are genuine, some of them rather rare. The Dolans don't have any children, which is sad because they've wanted them desperately for years.

Betsy said, "Hi," and I said, "Hi. How's the navel?" and Betsy said, "We're going into Harkness tomorrow, to get it vulcanized," and Tom said, "Oh, shut up. Thank God you're here. Now I have an excuse for a drink."

It seemed like a pleasant place to be on a rainy Sunday. "Kidneys," Tom said. "We're having kidneys and bacon for breakfast. After a little touch, of course. What'd you like, Deac? How about you, Twickenham?"

Twit-Twit gave him her little-girl's-eyes-batting, and Tom went on as if he had never asked a question. "There's only one sensible thing on a rainy Sunday morning—it is very cold champagne," which I knew he was going to say and was glad he did even though I don't greatly like champagne.

From the kitchen Betsy called, "Dolan hates champagne. Remember? Champagne is what he hates."

So Tom opened the bottle and poured its contents into four highball glasses and Betsy, from the kitchen, said, "God, what a bum."

Tom said, "You know, she's right. But I think I will just be a bum." He looked at his glass and drank a draught, and went on. "I think I'll be a bum because I enjoy the work, and the hours aren't bad."

"And you're the kid who can keep them," Betsy shouted.

"You can't really just be a bum and nothing else, can you?" Twit-Twit said. "Or can you?"

"Others have made it," Tom said. "Why can't I, a normal American boy?"

"And bums meet such interesting people," I said.

"Sure," said Tom. "Like you people."

"Sure," yelled Betsy. "Other bums." She came to the kitchen door to deliver the insult personally.

The wine was sharp and cold but the important thing was the feeling of being among friends.

From the kitchen Betsy called, "I'm starting to serve. Stand by!" There was a nice smell. Tom said, "We're having no orange juice." He waved his glass. "Only grape juice."

"Very nice," said Twit-Twit.

"I'll get some more," Tom said. "Champagne and kidneys go well together."

"How are yours standing up?" said Betsy, bringing in the plates.

"Very fine," said Tom. "Very fine." He thumbed the cork out of a second bottle of champagne. "After all, as the good poet said,

> *'Come, fill the cup, and in the fire of Spring*
> *Your Winter-garment of Repentance fling;*
> *The Bird of Time has but a little way*
> *To flutter—and the Bird is on the Wing.'"*

The kidneys smelled wonderful. There was brioche, and ragged, home-made bread, well-toasted and buttered, and coffee kuchen. The coffee was Continental, black and hot; Betsy's really a hell of a cook. Tom went on talking and gesturing wildly with the bottle.

"I hope that wine travels well," I said.

"Enjoy it while you can," Tom said, and poured.

"Not with this wonderful coffee," Twit-Twit protested.

"Then drink the wine first," said Tom. "After all, none of us is going to be here forever. Again, as the good poet said..."

"You already said what the good poet said," Betsy told him.

"You're damn right I did. And what is good enough for the good poet is good enough for me. But that's not the point."

"The point is," said Betsy, "there are other things to talk about."

"All I'm saying is, to cultured people like ourselves—well, anyway, like most of us—" He looked significantly at his wife.

*"Cultured,"* said Betsy with an intonation.

We went on eating and smiling.

"I'll bet you a thousand dollars no one here knows who Jan Mayen was," Tom said. "And he's on every map. Want to argue about culture?"

No one took the bet. He and Betsy wrangled amiably. It seems there's an island east of Greenland named after a guy or a ship named Jan Mayen, although it was originally discovered by the Danes and is inhabited mainly by foxes. Don't take my word for it; all this comes from Tom. When he can't sleep he reads the Encyclopedia Britannica. Betsy got more kidneys and coffee.

Presently I said, "Tom, what's all this about a dame on one of the shows named Low or Loewy? Used to be married to a guy named Brillhart?" Twit-Twit looked at me.

"Inez Low," said Tom. "That's not her real name, though."

"No?"

"No. Oddly enough, for someone in the music business, her real name is Lombardo. No relation to the Lombardo orchestra family of course. But they are so well known that years ago she decided she couldn't appear under her own name without sounding like an imitator, so she changed it to Low. She's a fill-in with us right now. I wouldn't know about her husband."

"Guy named Brillhart." I looked at Twit-Twit, telling her to shut up. "Song writer. Brill Brillhart, they call him."

"She was once pretty big," said Tom. "Not great but she had a name. Then she dropped out of the active side of the business and started coaching. She does know voice, I'll say that. Now she's back, or trying to get back as a singer. She's not as young as she used to be. Now that you mention it, I remember her saying the other night her ex-husband was in town. I guess he's been away. I don't know. Anyway, he'd paid her some dough she thought she'd have to sue him for, and she was happy. She'd got her coat out of hock, or something. You know how it is with entertainers."

While the women cleared the table and Tom fiddled with his hi-fi rig, I sat back on the davenport and closed my eyes. But I did not feel sleepy. I felt surrounded by Brillhart. He was dead but he was everywhere. Archie had heard he was alive. Twit-Twit and Tom had heard the same thing. His coat, hat and pipe had shown up, Kim Winter had seen him, Don Quayle had glimpsed him in the street. Eulalia had dated him and was dating him again tonight. His building superintendent had received a note from him, and I myself had talked to him on the phone.

But he was dead.

It was idiotic and impossible and uncanny. But it was happening.

And more of it would happen tonight, when Eulalia had her date.

I wanted to be on hand for that, but I also wanted to talk face to face with Rudolf Jersey. If I didn't waste time I could get out to the hospital and back this afternoon, before Eulalia's date.

"Duke Ellington at Newport" began its crashing, mounting excitement from the hi-fi. I went into the bedroom, closed the door, and telephoned.

"Doctors' and Nurses' Clinic," a nurse's voice said.

"Is there any chance of my seeing Mr. Jersey for a few minutes this afternoon if I come out? This is Mr. Pollock—" it was as good a name as any—"I'm an old friend." In a way Mr. Pollock *was* an old friend.

"I'm sorry, sir."

"Perhaps tomorrow?"

She hesitated. "You are a friend? Not a member of the immediate family?"

"That's right."

"Sir." A pause. "I am sorry to tell you Mr. Jersey passed away this morning."

I don't know what you say in a situation like that. What I said was, "I'm very sorry. Thank you. Good-by."

"Good-by, sir," the nurse said.

I reopened the bedroom door. Tom was saying, "Why don't I open another bottle of wine?"

"Really, we don't need it," Twit-Twit said.

"What's more, we can't afford it," Betsy said.

"Being poor is a great deterrent to immorality," said Tom.

"The only deterrent," I said.

We sat around for an hour talking, lazily and comfortably. Outside the rain was becoming sleet and it occasionally hit the dismal windows like handfuls of thrown slush. That turned out to be rather important.

# CHAPTER 9

## *The Shadow Dance*

It was a few minutes before seven when I found the stage door west of Broadway, told the doorman my name, and was nodded in. Out on the brilliantly lighted stage ahead of me Rise Stevens was singing an aria; beyond her, violinists were bending to her accompaniment, and other people stood around out of the cameras' range. One of them was Archie.

The aria ended to crackling applause and a man sitting at a desk in front of me started speaking the commercial eloquently, with an engaging cosmetic smile. Several visible clocks agreed it was forty-five seconds before seven o'clock. The cast moved forward, Indian file, for the last close-ups, then an arm waved, the music died in mid-measure, lights went out, and the people on stage dissolved in a mob. Archie caught sight of me.

Outside, I said, "We'd better hurry. Their date could have been for seven."

"But you know where to pick them up in case we miss them, you said."

"That's right. But I'd like to see this performance from the beginning."

"You think this is the windup?"

"It could be."

It was turning colder, and the sleet cast a whispering curtain over the Times Square signs and spread a treacherous gray carpet in the street on which our cab slithered and fishtailed, the driver swearing comfortably.

I had called Archie after dropping Twit-Twit off. At first I hadn't been sure I wanted him along but I'd decided that two were better than one on what would be a tailing job. When I called his apartment a low, pleasant woman's voice had answered. I assumed it was his fiancée. She said Archie was at the studio and would be until after the show and gave me the backstage phone number. You can tell a lot about people from their telephone manners, and Mary Brillhart Newton sounded nice and intelligent.

\* \* \* \*

Eulalia Pope lived in one of those small stylish new apartment buildings in the Thirties between Park and Madison and as we drove past I saw there was no doorman, at least not on Sundays. That was all to the good. At the Park Avenue end of the street I paid off the cab over Archie's protest.

"It'd be more comfortable, waiting in the cab," he said, shivering.

"And a lot more conspicuous. Eulalia and her date might even try to hail it. Now listen to this carefully. I am going to stay here. You take the Madison Avenue end of the street. They'll go one way or the other and leave either on foot or by car. The former is not very likely on a night like this, but in any case we play by ear. If they have a car we both scramble for a cab and the first to get one follows them. If it's on foot, the nearest one of us will follow them first—at a distance of a block at least, Archie. The second of us will follow the first, again from a distance of a block or two. Whatever you do, don't let your curiosity get the better of you and lead you to get too close to them. Even if you think you see Brillhart."

His gulp was almost audible.

"One last thing. If the two of them split up, you take Eulalia and I'll take the date. If we are separated, call me at home as soon as you can, and I'll call you at yours. Got it?"

He nodded and started solemnly for Madison. Eulalia's building had a well-lighted marquee of white canvas that made surveillance easy, and a house near Park had a below-street-level entrance that was nice and dark. I swung down into it, hoping that the family would not come home for a while and that the Thirteenth Precinct was not being especially vigilant tonight. I could imagine a desk sergeant's expression when I told him that I was merely tailing a dead man.

I stood there twenty minutes. A couple of pedestrians came by and didn't see me. The people who lived in the brownstone did not come home. Three people went into Eulalia's building, a middle-aged couple and a woman who had been walking her dog. No one came out. No one drove up. Staring down the street toward the white canvas hood, I told myself that the date could have been for 7:30 or more likely eight. I looked at my watch. It was 7:40. The sleet was becoming whiter and snowier and my feet were cold. I glanced at the traffic on Park occasionally. Empty cabs were going by. That was good.

It happened suddenly.

Maybe I had looked toward Park longer than a second. Anyway, there she was, standing under the bright canvas canopy a hundred feet from me, slender and chic in a striking vermilion wrap with white fur at the collar. Something glittered in her hair and also at her toes; she couldn't have been more noticeable had she been dressed in lighted neon tubing. She looked up and down the street as if expecting someone, and when a cab came through and pulled in automatically, she waved him on, and continued looking up toward my end of the street. Then, after another minute, she gathered her brilliant cloak around her and—incredibly!—began walking through the thick slush toward Madison. That made her Archie's quarry.

She turned north at Madison, a quick flash of red under the street light. Then—I was out on the sidewalk now—I saw Archie furtively leave his doorway and take off after her. *Not too close, fathead!* I started toward Madison.

Then something else happened.

I was walking slowly, figuring Archie would stay a block behind her and wanting to be at least one block behind him, and preferably two, for the street seemed empty. But the street wasn't empty at all.

A dark-coated woman had come from the other side of Madison and now, staying on the other side of the street from Archie and Eulalia, was walking after them, close to the buildings, clutching a large handbag. It was dark and the snow veiled everything a little, but I caught something catlike in the action. Was it all coincidence? As I reached Madison and saw how her pace timed itself to theirs, I knew it wasn't.

I waited until she was the best part of the block away. Archie was in the next block and Eulalia yet another block farther uptown, and still scintillant. It was quite a procession.

I stood for a moment, watching the woman immediately ahead to see if she looked back. She didn't. She clearly thought she had everything her own way—she was tailing the tailer.

Good. I'd tail her.

I crossed the street to be more directly behind her, took off and looked ahead.

Eulalia had disappeared.

Archie reached a corner, looked down each side street, then turned back toward Park, obviously going the way Eulalia had gone. I began to get an insane glimmering. I also began to close the gap between me and the lady I was following, who turned the corner Archie had turned.

An empty cab came by, its roof light a welcome beacon in the gloomy night. I waved it in violently. "Two blocks north," I said. "Fast! Then over to Park and stop."

I felt a little silly. "Private eye job," I said and hoped it sounded terse.

"Sure," said the cab driver. "Only two'll get you six you're checking on a girlfriend. You want it?"

"Wise guy!"

He chuckled. But when we got to Park he pulled up at the corner, switched off the lights and waited. I got out and looked down Park. Eulalia was not quite a block away walking toward me, head down in the sleet. There is something surrealistic about an attractive girl, all dressed up for a night club or party, slogging alone through slush and steady snowfall. Even as I looked, a southbound cab came by, slowed, honked and waited for her to hail it. She didn't.

Now I was sure. I ducked back and climbed into the cab.

In a moment Eulalia came around the corner and headed back toward Madison and my cab. In brief, she was walking around the block by herself on an impossibly unpleasant night, and when she went by my dark cab she looked awfully mad. I caught a glimpse of her open-toed shoes, the gold strapwork darkened by wet snow. Her feet must have been like icicles.

We waited. Archie came around the corner in a moment, looked about surreptitiously, didn't notice the cab, and started after her. When he got half-way down the block, the woman in the dark coat came around the corner. I got a glimpse of dark, fearful eyes and a determined face, the big pocketbook tightly gripped. Then she hurried on, closing the gap, and the possible danger that Archie was running—the curious and unpredictable danger—occurred to me with sudden force. Through the cab's rear window I had seen Eulalia cross Madison, look around and then turn south toward home. She was doubling back all right. I'd better get him out of it. That pocketbook probably held a gun.

What followed should have been a neat checkers game.

The light on Park turned green. "Take off," I told the cab driver. "Turn north, then west on Thirty-ninth. Stop this side of Madison."

He did, disregarding the red light at Thirty-ninth and making a skidding stop near Madison. I did not have to tell him to switch off his lights. I jumped out and looked cautiously down the avenue where Eulalia had turned. She was standing under a street light, and was looking around as if she wanted a cab. It was all clear as glass. She had made herself perfectly visible to the expected tail, completed her circuit of the block to give the other woman every chance to spot him, and now, the cold wet job done, was going home, frozen-footed.

It was simple. Archie would be standing in the same relative position as I at the street corner, but a block closer to her. The other woman would be a little behind him, awaiting his next move. She and Eulalia had staged a neat game of fox and hounds with an extra set of hounds. I was yet another set.

Then I caught my breath.

A man had appeared, out of nowhere, down the block, and was standing beside Eulalia. He was tall and big-shouldered. He wore an old, greenish trench coat and an Alpine hat with a feather in it. He took her arm. She smiled up at him; even at that distance I saw the flash of that pretty face under the street light.

Brillhart?

But Brillhart was dead.

He left her quickly, walked down the side street and out of sight.

I suppose it was the quick furtiveness of it that impressed me, or at least tended to convince me. If someone is putting on a masquerade they do it elaborately. But Brillhart, if that's who it was, had come out of the shadows only momentarily, had been barely glimpsable, and had then disappeared like the ghost of Hamlet's father. Even as my muddled brain registered these whirling thoughts, an elderly red MG roadster wheeled out of the side street, a block away, scooped up Eulalia and sped off down Madison.

Archie ran out from his corner and looked around wildly for a cab. Fortunately none was in sight. He began running toward my corner, since it was closer to Forty-second Street, hoping to find one. But halfway up the block he slowed down and gave up; he knew they had gotten away. He must have felt discouraged but also confused and also frightened if, as I gathered, he had gotten a fairly close-up look at Brillhart, or his double.

I ducked back to my cab and got in.

When Archie reached my corner, he turned and looked backward—for me, I suppose. If the other woman with the big handbag was in sight, he apparently did not notice her. Instead he turned left and walked the other way down Thirty-ninth Street toward a small neon sign I had not even noticed. *Dan's Do-Nut Shop.* His shoulders were hunched discouragedly but he plodded on with determination, and I liked him for it.

I watched him go into Dan's. As he did, the other woman came up, crossed the street, watched where he went, and then started after him. I could guess what he was going to do. I got out of the cab fast, handed the driver a $10 bill, said, "Wait here awhile," and began running toward Forty-second. If Dan's was in the telephone book—

I got to the all-night drugstore opposite Grand Central quite fast. I riffled the book, found Dan's Do-Nut Shop wasn't listed, swore, then realized I was looking in the Brooklyn book, found the Manhattan one, then Dan's, dialed it and got a busy signal. That was good. Archie was calling me, as I had figured. After a minute I tried again and a voice said, "Dan's Do-Nuts."

I described Archie and they called him to the phone. He said, "Hello?" guardedly.

"Listen, Archie."

"Deac?"

"Yes. Now listen. We're in a hurry. Look at your watch. In ten minutes a cab driver will go into that restaurant you're in and order black coffee. I'll tell him to rattle his spoon so you'll know him. When he finishes his coffee you engage him. You won't have to pay him anything—he'll know where to take you and he will be paid in advance. That's important."

"What's going on?"

"Never mind. He'll take you to Penn Station. Get out at once and hurry into the station—that's to lose the person following you. She'll be slowed up. She'll have to pay off her cab."

"I'm being *followed?*"

"Shut up. You know Penn Station?"

"Yes."

"Then when you get there move fast to another exit, grab a cab and get away from there. Start for Grand Central. If you have any doubts about whether you're followed, go on to Grand Central and do the same thing. Do it again at the Waldorf and then the Astor, if you have to. But you won't. Call me at home only when you know you're in the clear. But whatever you do, shake that tail—it's a woman in a dark coat. That's all I know. Got it?" Obediently he repeated the instructions. He had it.

I began to feel good. *We* were getting some cards to play, for a change.

Outside I flagged another cab, gave the driver $20 and told him how and where to rattle a teaspoon in a coffee cup. He looked happy about the whole thing and, what was more, he looked intelligent. I thanked whatever gods may be for the quick-witted New York cab driver. Now I had two of them working for me.

I hurried back to the first one at Thirty-ninth and Madison, feeling a little like the ringmaster in a circus. The woman who was following Archie was easy to spot because a trail of tracks in the new snow led to where she stood, a half-visible blur, between parked cars across from Dan's Do-Nut Shop.

I got into Cab Number One, told the driver what I wanted, gave him another $10—after all, this was Archie's money—as well as a card with my address and telephone number, and then waited, keeping an eye on my watch.

Well before the ten minutes were up the other cab pulled into the street, found a place to park and the driver went into Dan's as instructed. I got out of my cab. "Don't worry about a thing," the driver whispered after me. I walked away; it was out of my hands now.

But I couldn't help turning at the corner, and looking back.

Down the side street Archie and the other cab driver came out of the Do-Nut Shop, got into the cab and started toward Fifth. Immediately my cab lighted up, drove slowly toward the restaurant, and the woman, who had darted out into the middle of the street looking for a cab in which to follow Archie, saw mine coming and hailed it. They took off after the first cab. It had worked.

I walked up to Grand Central and took the subway downtown.

* * * *

In the apartment I replaced wet shoes with slippers, made some espresso, sat back and sipped the coffee while I waited for my telephone to ring. That gave me time to ask myself, since the mystery seemed pretty close to solution, why I had done all this for someone I hadn't seen in twenty years, who had never meant much to me, and who now could involve me in something rather unpleasant. I decided there were two reasons.

One was the puzzle itself. I have never liked the "How old is Ann?" kind of brain-twister, or checkers game problems, or crossword puzzles. But something untoward in real life, something inexplicable and strange—that draws me like a magnet.

The other reason was Archie's helplessness and appealing loneliness, as evidenced by the fact that he had no one else to turn to, with all his means, but a casual friend he had not seen since he was a helpless and lonely child.

This philosophizing was interrupted by Cab Driver Number One. He didn't phone; he appeared in person.

# CHAPTER 10

### *Coffee*

He was short and squat, with the grinning confidence of a man who knows that what he does is not vitally important but that he does it well. He wore a sports jacket, a sports-car cap, and a hearing aid.

"Hi," he said, and took off the cap. "I guess you're the party. I didn't get a good look at you before."

"I'm the party. Where'd you take her? And want some coffee?"

"That'd be fine. Well, I'll tell you." He sat down and I handed him coffee. "This was interesting, in a way."

"I'm very glad."

He sipped. "Good coffee. Now. You wanna know where she lives—right?"

"That was always the general idea."

"Right." He sipped again. "Well, I'll tell you. This dame really acted kind of odd. And at the end—well, I got a surprise for you. Or maybe you know who she is." He looked at me wisely over the coffee cup's rim.

The idea of hitting him with the espresso machine crossed my mind. "If I knew her name and address I wouldn't have hired you."

"Oh, sure. So I'll tell you from the beginning." He went on sipping his coffee and finally put the cup down.

"Why tonight?" I said. "Why don't you sleep on it and call me in the morning?"

He grinned, and extended the cup for more coffee. "Okay. My wife says the same. I talk too much. But you know what it's like, you're cooped up in a cab all day?"

"Sure. But why not tell me what it's like spying on a dame?"

"Okay. So she says follow that cab, like you told me she would, and they duck into Penn Station and I hold back a little like you said, to lose them. So by the time we get down the ramp where she can jump out, the other cab is long gone. So she said a few things to me a lady wouldn't have said and started to get out and then she gave me an address on East Fiftieth Street—"

"Number 199?"

"That's right. I thought you didn't know her?"

"Go on."

"Well, then she changed her mind and told me to drive her uptown. To West Seventy-first."

"And you did?"

"Sure. Good coffee."

"So you know where she lives."

"I sure do."

"If you'll tell me, I'll make some more coffee."

He laughed. "Where she lives is easy. She lives at 253 West Seventy-first. An old brownstone that's sort of an apartment, I figure."

"How do you know she wasn't just visiting there?"

"For two reasons. Because when she realized she'd lost the guy we were tailing, first she said to take her to Fiftieth. Then she says, no, she's changed her mind. 'Take me home,' she says. 'Okay, lady,' I says, 'where's home?' and she gives me the Seventy-first Street address. But the real kicker comes when I let her out. That's why I come down here in person. I figured you'd want to know this right away. Because that dame is famous."

I just waited, letting my coffee get cold.

"Yes, sir, famous. There's an old guy putting out a trash barrel in front of this address when we pull up, the manager or owner I suppose, and when he sees her, he comes over to help her out of the cab and he calls her by name. And you know who she is?"

I just looked at him.

"She's the wife of that famous old actor—you know, the Western star?"

"Who's that?"

"William S. Hart."

"How the hell do you know that?"

"That's who she is. That's what the manager calls her.

He opens the door and says very respectful—you know, 'Good evening, Mrs. Bill Hart.'"

"Are you sure he didn't say, 'Mrs. Brillhart'?"

"Maybe. But I doubt it. I'm old enough to remember Bill Hart, mister."

"Sure." But I began to feel better. It had worked.

"More coffee?"

"No, thanks. But since I got your phone number, you mind I have Laraine call you and find out what brand you use? She makes lousy coffee."

"Laraine?"

"My wife."

"Tell her to call any time."

"Thanks."

Just as he left the phone rang. I knew who it was.

Archie said, "I've got to talk fast—I'm home. What the hell happened? Where were you? God, Deac, do you know who I *saw?*"

"Did you see him—really? That's what I want to find out. I was around, all right. Closer than you thought. But was that Brillhart?"

I suppose he paused for only a few seconds, but it seemed like an hour.

"It *looked* like him," he said. "It really looked like him. It was dark and with the snow I couldn't see very well, but when he got under the street light, it sure looked like him. The only thing was he looked leaner."

He paused again. "But I guess he could have lost some weight, eh?"

"You're not absolutely sure it either was or was not Brillhart. Right?"

"Right." His voice was low and hesitant.

"Okay. Forget it. Get a good night's sleep. You did fine. We'll have this all cleared up within a day or so."

"You mean it?"

"I mean it. Everything's under control. Good night." Under control. Oh, brother!

# CHAPTER 11

*A Few in for Lunch*

When I set out next morning, most of the snow had disappeared, in the invisible way that snow vanishes from New York sidewalks. Only a little dirty rime here and there in the lee of a front step or along the curb was left to remind me of Eulalia's cold walk and the other woman's futile vigil.

Again I got into Brillhart's apartment without trouble. It was stuffy and I tried turning on the ventilating part of the air conditioner, but as Eulalia had said, it wasn't working. I looked around for a while, finding nothing new of importance except, in a drawer, some bills and opened letters, all postmarked within the past three weeks. Two letters were from a girl named Eden in Hollywood. She sounded hospitable.

There was coffee in a can in the kitchen and I made some. While it was percolating I called Quayle. As I expected, he sounded sleepy and, when I apologized and told him my name and where we'd met, politely disinterested.

"To come to the point," I said, "I'm a friend of Brillhart's, as you may have gathered. Some of us think he has turned up missing."

"In the last day or two?"

"Much longer than that. I can explain that but it'll take a lot of time. I'd rather just ask you one question. The other night at Kim Winter's you mentioned seeing Brillhart when you were passing the Music Hall some days ago. How sure are you it was Brillhart?"

"How sure do I have to be? It *was* Brillhart."

"How close were you to him?"

"Well, my cab was on the far side of Sixth from the Music Hall, if that's what you mean. He was in that old MG of his. On Fiftieth."

"And moving."

"Right."

"Did you get a good, full-face look at him?"

"Not at all. It was the—the general posture—you know what I mean. The car and the old raincoat."

"Then there's a fair chance it could have been someone else?"

"I suppose other people in New York have cars and coats like that. But why couldn't it have been Brill?"

"Maybe it was. Thanks a great deal."

That ended that. I waited awhile, then draped a handkerchief over the phone and dialed Kim Winter's number. A respectful Continental voice said, "Miss Winter's residence," and I said, "This is Mr. Brillhart. Miss Winter up yet?" Continental voice said she would see, sir. Waiting for her I also waited for the key's rattle in the front door that should come if I had correctly deduced the next move of the woman of last night.

Kim said, "Hello, Brill, you idiot," in my ear. She sounded like someone trying to sound mad, and not feeling mad at all.

"Look," I said. "I can explain everything. Come to my apartment for lunch."

"Why should I?"

"Because we have your future to talk over. Maybe I have news."

"Maybe! You louse! Where in the world have you been?"

"Twelve-thirtyish," I said. "And if you're delayed or anything, call me, will you? I'm at home." That was the clincher, in case my voice made her suspicious.

Then I called Eulalia and said somewhat the same thing. I got a considerably warmer reception, so I let my voice get intimate too. She said she'd come for lunch. Then I called Archie.

"Western Union just called," Archie said.

"What about?"

"A telegram—what do you think?" It was the irritableness of gnawing alarm. "It was from Brillhart. He invited me to dinner. At his apartment. Tomorrow night."

I chuckled. "You won't have to go. Instead, come to lunch at his apartment today, at twelve-thirty, and learn the solution to your mystery at first hand."

"Do you mean it?"

"Sure. And don't worry about that telegram. It wasn't from Brillhart."

There was a silence. "You know who sent it to me?"

"Don't lean on me too hard. I don't know everything. But I'll bet you meet the sender soon."

"I'd better come alone?"

"It might be as well."

Now there was nothing to do but wait. One thing was sure. I didn't have to get any lunch ready.

\* \* \* \*

It was a quarter after twelve, and I was getting a little worried, when a key sawed into the lock. I glided to the bedroom closet from which, I had already made sure, I could see into the living room. The door opened, a woman pulled the key from the lock, and walked in. She moved with leisurely confidence, not surreptitiously; she didn't expect a challenge. She was the woman of last night.

She took a man's pipe and a fold of musical manuscript from her large purse and put them on the table. Then she sniffed critically, shrugged and started for the door. I stepped out of the closet.

"Hello, Mrs. Brillhart."

She gave a shriek and put a stifling hand to her mouth. I got between her and the front door and had my first good look at her.

Her large dark eyes, wide with fear, had once been beautiful; now they wore the heavy, black-crust make-up with which some women try to disguise forty years. The face itself still had its roundly youthful contours and there was a self-conscious chic and poise about her that, even in a moment of alarm, suggested stage experience.

"Who are you?" Her lips remained parted appealingly, but hard suspicion narrowed the mascara-lined eyes.

"My name's Bill Deacon. I've been waiting all morning for you. I figured you'd show up since you started for here last night."

I heard her breath suck in.

"I see you were returning the props. I don't think you'll need them again. You *are* Mrs. Brillhart?"

"Don't call me by that filthy name!"

"Oh, yes. Sorry, Miss Low. Your husband never really did enable you to get your fur coat out of hock, did he?" Again the look of alarmed surprise; she was getting a taste of her own medicine. "In fact, you haven't seen him for quite a while. But that black cloth one is pretty, and good for shadowing, eh? Why not take it off and sit down? We have lots to talk over and your friends Eulalia and Kim will be here any moment." That jarred her too.

"And—my ex-husband?"

"He won't."

"Where is he?" Then she corrected herself—"Where is the slimy bastard?"—so that I would not take it for concern.

"All in good time." The doorbell rang and I pressed the button. "What makes you dislike him so?"

"Because he showed me what a fool I could be, just as he is showing Eulalia and Kim Winter what fools they are. His only interest in a woman is how much he can get out of you."

"You mean money?"

"I mean money, I mean love, I mean as steppingstones—anything!" Her eyes flashed, her voice became guttural.

There was a knock, I admitted Kim Winter; she looked big and shouldery in a tweed coat. She also looked surprised. The bell rang again and I pressed the button again.

I waved Kim into the living room and waited by the open door. I wanted to ask my questions, not answer theirs.

"What's going on?" I heard Kim murmur.

"I don't know."

"What's he doing here? Where's Brill?"

"He's going to tell us. He thinks he knows everything."

"You mean even—" The rest was a whisper.

"He may," Inez replied in a normal tone.

Eulalia stepped off the elevator and brushed past me with a "Hi," went on in, called "Brill?" got no answer and looked at the others. "Where's Brill?" I began feeling like a card player who's shaken too many aces out of his sleeve.

Inez was lighting a cigarette. "Ask *him,*" Kim told Eulalia.

I said, "In a moment. One more guest is arriving."

"Brill," said Eulalia. Her face was, as the song goes, the face of a woman in love.

"Not Brill." Something in my voice arrested all their eyes.

"What do you mean—where is he?"

I merely held up a hand in what I hoped looked like confidence. But I was nervous. I'd drawn up the best plan I could devise and I had had the advantage of choosing the time and place of attack. Even so, it was a tricky assault, postulated on guesses, depending on bluff and vulnerable to counterattack. Where was Archie?

He arrived just as the silence was changing from heavy to unbearable.

"Now we're assembled," I began brightly. "I'm afraid I got you here under false pretenses. There'll be no lunch. But there's coffee, if you're famished."

No one was interested in coffee. They were interested in me, though.

"I'm not sure whether you three have broken any laws by the act you've been putting on," I began. "You may have." I knew they hadn't. "One thing is certain. You are guilty of disturbing the peace—the peace of mind of a number of people. I know *why* you did it. But who started it?"

Four pairs of eyes looked up at me. No one answered.

"Don't want to tell?"

"What have we to tell?" asked Kim.

"Why tell anything?" demanded Inez.

"For that matter, why should I tell you? But I'm going to. Some two months ago Brill Brillhart disappeared. A lot of people either didn't notice it or didn't care, for a lot of people didn't like him. But you three, for different, highly personal reasons, did care. And you knew how much he was disliked. Perhaps for that reason, as the weeks passed, you began to suspect foul play."

"It was more than suspecting," said Inez.

"Yes? Want to explain that?"

A shrug.

"Okay. Somehow you had got the idea that he had—well, run into trouble. And, as I read it, it went like this. You, Miss Low, wanted to find your ex-husband because he owes you money. You, Miss Pope, because you are in love with him. You, Miss Winter, because of some affection perhaps, but mainly because he represented, as your voice coach, your best chance for a singing career. And you all had reasons for believing that if he had not met with foul play you would have heard from him.

"Miss Low, he's owed you money for a long time. You had threatened to sue him, and he couldn't run out on that debt permanently—by the very nature of his work as song writer and musician he must be before the public, and in its good graces." Her dark, strong face was a brooding Buddha's.

"As for you, Miss Pope, you were similarly confident Brillhart would not have run out—"

"I *know* he wouldn't," she cried tremulously. "He loved me!" (A gleam of amused contempt lighted the Buddha face.) "I'm sure—*sure*!—something terrible has happened." She was close to tears.

"I see. Now, Miss Winter, I'll admit I'm guessing a little here, but I'd assume you would promise Brillhart a fair sum if he coached you into a singing success. True or false?"

"True."

"Five thousand dollars, maybe? Ten? Not that it's any of my business."

She looked defiantly at the other women. "Ten."

"And you know Brillhart is not the type to run voluntarily away from ten thousand dollars. To sum up, all three of you had different reasons for wanting to find Brillhart if he was alive, and for suspecting foul play if he wasn't. Whose idea was the charade?"

"Where's Brill, if you know so much?" demanded Eulalia.

Kim's over-plucked eyebrows arched quizzically.

That was the question I wanted to avoid—if possible. "You all knew each other," I went on. "You had a common interest in Brillhart's whereabouts, if for different reasons. Little wonder that you finally got together, and that someone came up with an idea. Who?"

Rebellious silence. But Eulalia's involuntary nod indicated I was on the right track.

"It was an ingenious idea. I suppose you made up a list of suspects on which Mr. Sinclair here would naturally appear since he and Brillhart had once had...a...a public encounter. Or perhaps you simply began the play, so to speak, and carefully watched everyone within earshot to see who might be affected. The plot in any case was simple. You would all three, co-operatively, behave as though Brillhart was actively around, that you were seeing him regularly, dating him, inviting him, and in one case getting money from him. As his estranged wife Inez Low still had, or was able to obtain, a key to his apartment, on which you kept the rent paid—by mail. Inez, if I may use first names, supplied the props. Not the original hat and trench coat, which had disappeared with Brillhart, but good imitations. And the pipe, and even the forged letter referring to the musical Brillhart supposedly wrote and which helped explain his absence from Kim's party. In all this you had, at one point, the unknowing co-operation of Don Quayle, who reported seeing Brillhart near Radio City Music Hall."

"Didn't he?" That was Inez.

"He thinks he did. However, to finish up: the simple beauty of your scheme was that to the many who would have no idea that Brillhart had disappeared, everything you said would make perfect sense. But to someone with guilty knowledge—wow! He'd feel he was haunted and sooner or later he'd show it.

"Well, you played your roles—Eulalia even tested me—you gradually assembled a list of suspects, and laid a trap for them."

"Wrong," said Inez.

"The hell it's wrong! The climax of the scheme called for Eulalia, a natural choice, to advertise to everyone she met a forthcoming date she was to have with Brillhart, on the ground that, if anything would make a guilty person come forward, it would be a chance to see whether his 'victim' was up and walking around. You arranged for her to leave her apartment conspicuously so that, if she were tailed, another of you—Inez—could tail the tailer and thus find out who he was. A neat trap. As the tallest of the three, Kim even put on man's clothes and played Brillhart, to jolt the guilty thoroughly. Anything wrong with that reasoning?"

"Nothing," said Kim Winter. "Except one thing. Most of the suspects eliminated themselves quickly. One did not. That was Archie Sinclair here. Eulalia first spotted him in Clarke's when she did the bit. I asked him to a cocktail party, tested him—and he reacted like a startled deer. Besides, he was a good friend of Rudolf Jersey's and we knew Brill was having a business date with Jersey about the time he disappeared."

That was the admission I was waiting for. Now it was time to make my move. I'd solved the mystery of Brillhart's return from the grave and I didn't like Archie's obvious guilty alarm.

I chuckled confidently. "Certainly you don't think that Archie Sinclair did away with Brillhart! You know him, Miss Winter—and quite well. Is he the kind of man to resort to violence?"

"Then why did he follow Eulalia last night? What was his interest?"

Archie jumped and Eulalia said, "Yeah, why?" at the same time.

"And," said Inez, "what's your own interest in all this?"

I gave them an indulgent smile. "Maybe it's time *we* did a little explaining." I spoke to Archie, hoping to get the fearful look off his face. I did not succeed. "Mr. Sinclair and I are old schoolmates. When he recently found himself in a strange predicament he enlisted my help. For the fact is—and I am now telling you something in confidence—" I looked at each in deadly seriousness—"the fact is, Mr. Sinclair recently became engaged to Brill Brillhart's sister, Mary Newton. And the fact is he once had trouble with Brillhart. And the fact also is, as you well know, that wherever he has gone recently he has heard the name of Brill Brillhart mentioned and has received news of Brillhart's activities. Now, it so happens that Mr. Sinclair is rather wealthy, and a somewhat quiet...ah...withdrawn, studious man."

I looked again at Archie, encouragingly. He was crouched in his chair, like a coiled spring.

I hurried on. "Frankly, knowing Brillhart's character, Mr. Sinclair suspected that his fiancée's brother might be trying some extortion or blackmail scheme, of which these were just the preliminaries. I know it sounds farfetched. But he is a musician and not versed in practical matters. That is why he came to me for help and that is why I advised him to pretend to be falling for whatever was going on and even to follow Miss Pope last night, as I gathered he was intended to do."

I had to slide over that rather fast.

"You see, I am really to blame for what he did last night. Because, while neither of us knew what was going on, after a little thought I began to see a pattern in it. I think it came to some kind of absurd climax this morning when one of you sent a telegram to Mr. Sinclair in Brillhart's name, asking him—a man with whom Brillhart once had a fight—to dinner here. Idiotic!"

"Eulalia's idea," said Kim scornfully. "No doubt that's what gave it away."

"No, it was given away much earlier. One thing that made me wonder, early in the game, was the large number of traces left by Brillhart. A man doesn't normally leave so many indications of himself around when making visits—pipe, coat, hat, letters, music, and the like. Not to mention phone calls—I assume, Inez, that was your deep contralto I conversed with on the phone at Kim's, since with your voice training you'd be the one best qualified to imitate a man. But you all planted the clues a little too thickly to be convincing, especially since this apartment shows no indications of having been actually lived in recently.

"Then consider how many people had *not* seen Brillhart who should have. The apartment caretaker, and his music publisher, although he mistakenly thought he had. No one had heard of the new movie he was supposed to have scored—no one but you three. And the score itself turned out to be nothing new—but a collection of old Brillhart rejects, plus one really good song that he had not written, as I happen to know.

"Actually, all this had a pattern. Brillhart was heard but not seen, often heard of but never met, absent-minded about his belongings but remarkably careful never to be present in the flesh. And who always reported seeing him, meeting him for dates, and produced his belongings? Only three people. You three.

"When I put the two sets of facts together and thought of the strong motives you each had for wanting to know where he might be, I came to the rather obvious conclusion that he was indeed missing and that you were playing a kind of game in an effort to get a clue. I also concluded—and this was always my main purpose—that Mr. Sinclair's fears about a plot against his future happiness were groundless. Q.E.D."

I stole a glance at Archie. He looked a little recovered. The three women looked fairly credulous.

"Well, Archie, that clears up the mystery—eh? Let's be on our way."

"Just a minute," said Inez. "Why'd you ask everyone over here especially? Why'd we have to meet here? How'd you get in?"

"The caretaker. And because I knew an invitation like this would bring everyone without fail. Coming, Arch?"

He had been listening with terrible intensity, yet now he did not hear me. He was like a catatonic. Then he spoke. First he licked his lips, started out huskily, coughed, and began again. "Why—" he said. "Why do you suspect—foul play?"

Shut up, you dumbbell!

Inez's dark eyes narrowed. Eulalia looked puzzled. But Kim drawled an unconcerned answer.

"Because Inez got a message from Brill. From beyond the grave, so to speak. On a Ouija board." She spoke contemptuously; she did not want to associate herself with such medievalism. "Brill told her he had been murdered." But the effect on Archie was devastating.

*"Murdered!"* He uncoiled from his chair and advanced wildly on me. "They know about it!"

As though the vibrations in his voice had started the motor, the air conditioner I had fooled with earlier suddenly began to hum a high stridency.

Up to that time point we'd gotten away with it.

# CHAPTER 12

### *The Last Line of Defense*

"Of course we know," said Inez instantly. She was too fast to be comfortable.

All there was to do now was stall, try to cover Archie's break, and give him a chance to recover the wits he'd lost completely. "What bunk are you handing us?" I didn't care whether what I said made any sense as long as it distracted them. "Have you completely flipped? What is it you think you know?"

"What does *he* know?" said Inez. "What is it he's so afraid we have learned?"

"God knows," I said. "When we reach the point where we're putting our faith in messages from beyond the grave I bow out. This was supposed to be a meeting of sane people."

"It is," said Kim. "Don't get any wrong ideas."

"So you believe in Ouija."

"I didn't really believe it when Inez first came to us with it. Neither did Eulalia. But we were both greatly concerned about Brill."

"Come to you with what?"

"Brill's message. That he had been murdered."

I looked at Inez. "Do you care to try to explain that?"

She looked anger at me, but she looked venom at Kim. That was good.

"It is not so hard to explain." The emotional guttural was back. "I have used Ouija for years. You may laugh—most people do. Like Kim and Eulalia. But time and again it has given me advice that was sound and—and prophetic. For many years. I always consult it before a decision, always. My father has spoken to me through it." She looked aggressively at us, and we waited with curious respect.

"One night late in January I could not sleep so around three o'clock I got out the Ouija board. I didn't know why I did it, though I know now. Brill was calling me. I sat a long time by the window, before the table began to move over the board, taking my hands with it involuntarily. You do not know what it is like, that communication."

I didn't. But I could envision her sitting in a still, shadowy room in her nightdress waiting for a message—what message? From where? And it came, or so she believed, and from the dead. I could feel my flesh crawl.

"Finally Brill began to speak to me through the board. He identified himself and said he was dead, and had been for several weeks. He said he had been murdered. He—he seemed very emotional. The table moved violently at times. He said his body lay far away. I tried to ask for details but he would not answer me."

"And you are sure it was Brill?" I asked.

"He referred to things only he and I know about."

In spite of its absurdity in daylight, her story had cast a spell over the room. Her Ouija results were easily explained, of course. She hated Brillhart and desired his death, consciously or otherwise. So her subconscious, operating the little table, told her he was dead and convinced her of it with "things only he and I know about."

Yet she awed us all, in the midst of the bright sunshine and the traffic murmur.

Archie asked, "Did—did he tell who murdered him?"

"No."

But she was watching him carefully and quickly amended her answer. "That is, not exactly. I spoke to him only once." Then she twisted the knife. "But I'll speak to him again." Her smile glittered malice. "I'll hear from Brill. You may, too."

Even Archie's nose was white with fear.

I said, "Do you mean this whole rigmarole is based on a Ouija board session?"

"Not entirely," said Kim. "I'll admit, as I said, that neither Eulalia nor I put much faith in what Inez told us. We're not—superstitious, or whatever it is. But we did know that Brill seemed to have disappeared. He was a Bohemian and certainly an individualist, of course, and he could have just decided to pull up stakes or even"—she looked directly at Eulalia—"found a new girl with money. He was good at that. But Brill was always a guy you heard about, if not from. As the days passed, we wondered. Then Inez came up with another idea, which sounded better than the Ouija board. Want to tell them, Inez?"

Inez answered confidently. "In my grandfather's village in Italy when a crime was committed the authorities sometimes played a paisano trick to get a confession. Everyone was assembled in the church and then they made it appear that one of the statues—an image of a saint—was talking to the congregation about the crime and what a terrible thing it was, and the hell-fire that would punish the guilty. It seemed like a miracle and it seldom failed to frighten the guilty person so that he gave himself away. I told Kim and Eulalia that we could work a variation of it."

"Very clever," I said. "You certainly created a mystery for a while, even if it didn't work otherwise. Well, let's be getting on, Archie. You're overdue at the studio."

But as Archie rose, so did Inez. A little smile like summer lightning flickered over her dark saturnine face. "What do you mean, it didn't work?" she said softy. "I think it did work. I don't think you will laugh at Ouija again, my wealthy young friend," she told Kim vindictively. Then she turned to Archie. "Why were you so interested in learning whether Brill named his murderer? Why did you get so nervous when you heard Brillhart was still around? Why did you really follow Eulalia last night?"

"Come *on,* Archie! You're late now." I took his arm.

"Is it because you know who killed him?"

Never have I seen a man look as he looked at her. It wasn't a man. It was panic personified.

"Or is it because you—you killed him?"

For a second everyone was motionless, straining toward some unforeseen climax.

"No," Archie whispered. "I didn't kill him. But I know—I know he's dead."

Eulalia's scream shrilled round the walls, she twisted in torment and began to weep hysterically. Inez leaned forward intently and demanded with dark suspicion, "How do you *really* know?"

Kim uttered a gasp, unexpectedly produced a tiny handkerchief, and began to dab at her eyes. Brillhart had two mourners, at least. But this was no time for irony. I was at my last line of defense.

"Very well," I said. "You've forced our hand. Bear in mind that we tried not to have to tell you this, and it was out of respect for the dead. There's no point in raking up ancient scandals, especially when all concerned are past human punishment. For the fact is that Brillhart is indeed dead—he was killed under disgraceful circumstances. By an old and tragic man, out of justifiable revenge. And the old man is dead."

So at last I told them, in condensed form especially as to Archie's part in it, the story of Brillhart's murder. It was a strangely quiescent gathering, like the survivors of a disaster, when I finished. This was the turning point.

"You swear this is true?" asked Inez.

"To the best of my knowledge and belief, it certainly is."

"Then we've got to go to the police," said Kim.

Eulalia was looking at me, hating me for what I'd said as much as if I had caused it to happen.

"That's where we're going," she said. "The police." She was a white, tearful wraith, bereft of her lover, wanting only vengeance.

"Are you?" I said. "With what?"

They looked at me. "All you've got to go on is what I told you. That's hearsay and not admissible as evidence in court. And I got it from someone else—double hearsay. And he got it from Jersey—that makes it triple hearsay. And Jersey is dead." This was the last line of defense.

"So you say," said Kim.

"It was on the eight-o'clock news this morning," said Inez.

"What do you think the police, or any law court, can do about this? Of course, you can go to the police. That will put it in all the papers. But what else will it do, except help the tabloids' circulation? Brill Brillhart is dead—you can't bring him back to life. You can publicize an ugly, disgraceful story about him, though. If you want to blacken the name of a dead man you like, or once liked, go ahead. You won't accomplish anything else. You can't gain any revenge—there's no one to revenge yourself on."

I was registering with Kim and Eulalia, at least. "Besides, you'll have to explain to the cops why you were so interested in this and how you arranged the elaborate act. That means it will all come out—how Brillhart was involved with all of you and played each one for what he could get. Want that in the papers?"

I watched it hit home and turned on Inez. "You stand to inherit his estate, for you're still his wife. But how much a police investigation might complicate things I can't say. It might be years before—"

Inez was quick when it came to money. "Sure," she said. "But so far he's only missing. It takes seven years for a man to be proven legally dead. I don't want to wait seven years. What about—about his body?"

"Oh, what about that?" cried Eulalia piteously.

"That's the point," I said. "I think it's been found. There was a newspaper story recently. And if it hasn't been found, it soon will be. It must. Then"—this to Inez—"all you have to do is to let legal procedure take its course, and everybody's in the clear."

Inez nodded. The last defense was holding. Eulalia began, "But...but... we can't just—"

Kim's big, strong-fingered hand closed over hers kindly. "Yes, we can, honey. Because we've got to. He's right. There's nothing we can do except get all of us in a mess—a mess of bad publicity. After all, we have careers to think of, don't we? At least let's agree to wait until the body is found. Then we can decide what we ought to do—if anything."

I took my first full breath in an hour.

Everyone stood up. The mystery of Brillhart's resurrection was solved. Archie was in the clear. Rudolf Jersey's name was unblemished, at least publicly.

We left the apartment as soon as the three women had gone. As a parting gift I left the passkey on a table for the caretaker. Then I went on to the office.

# CHAPTER 13

## PHONE CALL

You could say the story ended here.

You could say that if you didn't care what you said.

Archie and Mary Brillhart Newton were married a week later in a civil ceremony at City Hall. Twit-Twit and I, the Dolans, and a few friends of the bride's attended. Later we went to the St. Regis for champagne toasts and Tom Dolan had a lot of champagne.

"Some people cry at weddings," said Betsy. "Our boy Tom doesn't. He gets plastered."

"It's because weddings are morbid," Tom said. "A prelude to disaster."

Betsy called him something.

"Besides, I had to toast the bride," said Tom. "She's pretty."

"She's more than pretty," said Twit-Twit. "She's wonderfully attractive."

They were right. Mary Brillhart Newton was pretty in the womanly, understanding, placid-browed way that you don't often encounter these days. Judging from the photograph I'd seen of her brother, she looked somewhat like him. But where Brillhart's good looks were of the craggy, aggressive-profile sort, this feminine version was softer, wiser, and compassionate. This is a quality that goes beyond mere prettiness, and the first time I met her I quickly realized how much she must mean to Archie. She was calm and loving and maternal and Archie was lonely and shy and helpless.

After the wedding reception Twit-Twit and I drove them in his car up to his apartment to gather their things. While the women busied themselves in the bedroom before the mirror, Archie and I stood talking in the big living room with its view up the sun-stippled Hudson. Suddenly he clapped his hand to his face.

"Oh, Lordie! Getting married has been too much. Deac, do me one last favor?"

"Sure. What?"

He went to a closet in the hall and began rummaging through coats hanging there. "Not that you've not done enough already." He brought out a silver flask. There were three bullet holes in it.

"It's the last trace of Brillhart," he whispered. "I've been going to get rid of it for weeks. But in the general excitement I forgot. I don't want to take a chance on Mary—you know what I mean."

"I'll take it."

I looked at it curiously. There were three holes on one side of it but only two, plus an outward dent, on the other side. I shook it experimentally and heard a leaden rattle. "One slug never got through both sides of it," I said. It was a strange souvenir of a man's death. I slipped it into my pocket.

Archie said, "You don't know what it's meant, having you when I needed you. If I can ever—"

"Forget it. Have fun in the Caribbean."

We went with them in a cab to the ship, bade them bon voyage, then had dinner on Mulberry Street. I don't know whether it was the antipasto, or the rite of seeing them off, or just the wedding. But Twit-Twit was wonderfully easy to get along with that night.

* * * *

I disposed of the flask the next day. It wasn't necessary but I pasted adhesive tape over the holes, filled it with sixty cents' worth of BB's from a hardware store, wrapped it in a few pages of newspaper, then walked over to the docks at the end of West Forty-eighth Street. I dropped the paper into the river and caught the quick gleam of silver in the murky water as the flask slipped out of its wrapping after it hit the surface. That was that.

Two weeks went by; we got several cards from Mary and Archie—St. Thomas, Trinidad, Barbados. I started a story on some new techniques for recording sound that took me up to Stamford each day for a week. That is how I happened to see this flask as I was passing through Grand Central one night.

There were a lot of them in one of those cutlery and gadget shops but I had no trouble in spotting this one. It had a kind of pebbled silver finish and was a duplicate in every way of the one I had disposed of. I bought the flask on impulse. Perhaps I was influenced by the careful laboratory methods of the sound engineers I'd been dealing with. Perhaps it was a kind of subconscious reasoning.

Two days later I borrowed a .38 from a deputy police inspector I know, went down into the basement, and set the flask on some boxes, backed by pine boards. I carefully emptied the gun into it from a distance of about four feet. It made a lot of noise and a woman upstairs complained, but it wasn't heard out on the street.

Then I examined the flask. What I saw bothered me.

The Sinclairs, as I might as well start calling them, telephoned me on the day they got back to New York. They wanted Twit-Twit and me to have dinner with them, and they sounded healthy and sunburned, even on the phone. But Tom Dolan had four tickets for an off-Broadway show he wanted to scout for TV and I begged off. The play was a dog and we were all glad enough to have a nightcap afterward and go our separate ways. I took Twit-Twit home and then, because it was a nice April night, I started walking down Fifth Avenue.

I walked all the way home, which is why I didn't get in until 1 a.m. When I did, the phone was ringing.

A low, hoarse voice grated something in my ear. I said "What?" irritably.

"Deac!" the voice rasped. "Is this Bill Deacon?"

"Sure."

"It's me—Archie. Can you hear me? I'm talking from the bedroom."

"Sure. But—"

"You've got to come out at once."

"What's the matter?"

"Brillhart."

"What?"

"Deac, I am going insane. I must be. But it's Brillhart!"

"Who is? Or what is? Speak up."

"I can't. Listen. Drop in just as though it were a late social call. I can't let Mary or him know I've called you."

"Archie, what the hell are you talking about?"

His husky whisper rose like a subdued shriek. It was terrifying.

"It's Brillhart!" he cried. "He's alive! He's not twenty feet from me at this moment in the living room, laughing and talking to his sister. Christ, don't you understand? He looks white and half-dead but it's Brillhart!"

Maybe I'm overly emotional. My hand holding the phone began to shake. Something like a graveyard worm started down my back.

# THE LATER TRACES

"...It is very curious and complex, Watson."

"Why should you go further in it? What have you to gain from it?"

"...This is an instructive case. There is neither money nor credit in it, and yet one would wish to tidy it up."

—Conan Doyle: *The Adventure of the Red Circle*

# CHAPTER 1

## *The Dead Man*

There was an empty cab parked at Sixth Avenue, a lucky thing at that time of night. "Get on the West Side Highway and go like hell north," I said. "I'll give you the address when I think of it." The driver grunted.

I lay back on the bouncing seat and tried to reason, which I am not very good at. I didn't believe for a moment that Archie was insane. Therefore Brillhart at this very moment was in the Sinclairs' living room, talking to his sister, and a terrified Archie needed help. Therefore Jersey had not killed Brillhart. I thought of my experiment with the flask. Therefore...

The driver drove with a heavy foot; still we seemed to barely crawl past Riverside Drive's monoliths. It was 1:23 when we pulled up before the new, chaste apartment building. When I pushed the button opposite Sinclair I got an instant response. Upstairs, Archie stood at the open door to his duplex.

"What goes on?" I whispered. "Tell me what I'm supposed to be doing here."

He answered in an intended-to-be-overheard voice, "Hi, Deac. Glad you saw our light. We've been listening to a fascinating story."

And he led me into the living room.

Mary gave me a bright smile and a big, tweedy broad-shouldered man got out of his chair. "Deac," said Archie, "this is Mary's brother, Brill Brill-hart."

I took a deep breath.

In the chair he had been in shadow; getting up, smiling, extending a hand, his face caught a lamp's side light and I got my first look.

He was a tall, bulky man with a fleshy face that was pale and lined in a way bespeaking convalescence. Yet it was still strong and virile, even of feature and alert of eye. A lock of curly, dark-blond hair fell picturesquely over his forehead; he transferred a highball to shake hands, confidently, shook the hair lock back and, as intended, it did not stay. His sports jacket was old and worn, the tie loosely knotted, the whole effect one of handsome Bohemian-ism. This was Brillhart.

I tried to act like someone who'd just dropped in, and had never heard of Brillhart, and was going to stay only a minute.

"Brill, you've really got to tell Deac your story," said Archie and gave me a look. "I've never heard anything more astounding."

Brillhart smiled confidently, a man accustomed to astounding people.

"Well, I'll admit," he said in a baritone vibrant with stage training, "I never heard of anything like it, at least so close to New York."

"Furthermore," Mary said, "Deac's a magazine writer. He might be interested in writing about it."

The smile died; Brillhart's glance became businesslike. "It's crossed my mind that this could make a walloping magazine story," he said. "What would I be likely to get out of it?"

I said, "That's hard to say, without knowing what the story's about."

"Ten thousand or so though, eh? At least?"

"Maybe. Depending, as I said, on the story."

"Don't worry about that. When you hear what I've been through—well, I can guarantee you, Deacon, you've never heard such a story as this one."

I have heard remarks like that so often they nauseate me.

"On the other hand, I'm relying on you as a friend of Archie's not to steal what I may tell you." The nausea stopped and I began getting mad.

"Really, that is hardly necessary," said Mary.

"Sure, sure. Still, if you knew the double-crossing that goes on in the music business... Okay, we're all friends. Briefly, Deacon, it's like this. I got back into town tonight, after three months and more of being out of this world—really out of this world! Part of it, close to death. But always out of touch with everything. For instance, I got here broke—I hitchhiked in—call Mary at her old digs and find she's married, for gosh sake. I call another friend, to float a small loan until I can get to a bank and learn I'm supposed to have written a score for a new Hollywood musical. Hell! Maybe they have picked up some of my things at that. They could do worse, I promise you. But you see what I mean. For three months I've been—"

"Why don't you start at the beginning?" I said.

"Sure. Good idea. Well, as I was saying. About three months ago a certain man in the music business called me up—I'm leaving his name out now because tomorrow I'm going around to see him. And that's for sure! If he listens to reason, there'll be no story—no publicity at all. If he doesn't—how about another round, Arch boy?"

He held up his glass and Archie rose like a trained spaniel. This was quite a guy. We had just met but Brillhart was already incorporating me in his scheme to blackmail Rudolf Jersey, not knowing that Jersey was dead.

"Thanks, Arch. Well, this old guy I'm referring to and I wrote a show years ago." He sipped his fresh drink. "It was a flop—I'm being perfectly honest. The book stank and the music was lousy. Maybe my lyrics weren't as good as they would be if I wrote them today—we all improve with time. Still, some people were nice enough to say the lyrics were the only good thing in it. Anyway, it folded, and I forgot it. That's how you have to operate in the music business—you roll with the punches or you go nuts.

"Then late in December this character calls me up and wants to see me. He hints he wants my help with another show. Well, you know how it is—I'm always pretty busy, but this guy is old and needs help. So one night I go to see him. And I discover he's crazy.

"He's been brooding about this flop we wrote years ago and after we're comfortably seated he says he blames me for its failure. I reason with him but he pulls a gun and says he's going to kill me. Ever have a gun pulled on you? This was my first time, and I don't want any more! I can still remember the crazy look in his eyes."

For the moment, I recognized, he was telling the truth.

"I tried to get out of my chair—he pulled the trigger—I—Christ!"

"Easy, dear," his sister said.

"It isn't easy to tell how—you were killed," he said, and I knew the moment of truth was not over.

"I don't remember any more," he went on. "When next I became conscious it was early morning or twilight, I don't know which. I was lying on my face in some woods. It was awfully cold and there was a stink of whiskey. Somebody rolled me over—a man. He looked crazy, too. He talked to someone else but I was beat and my chest hurt. They seemed to be arguing. Finally, two of them made a stretcher with jackets and branches, and picked me up and I passed out."

He paused to take a long pull at his glass, and I thought of the experiment with the flask. I'd been right in my misgivings. The flask had been heavy enough to save Brillhart's life because it had stopped at least one of the bullets in the heart area and slowed the others enough to prevent great penetration. I took little pleasure in this confirmation of my suspicions, for I was too concerned with what was coming next, and Brillhart had started talking again.

"When I came to I was in a low-ceilinged room, like an attic, and a woman was doing something to my chest with cloths. When I tried to talk a pain went through my chest. I'd wake up and then pass out again. Sometimes there was a little daylight from a small window in the roof, sometimes there was a kerosene lamp.

"Sometimes the woman woke me by doing something with the bandage. Occasionally she brought me some sort of tea and gave it to me by spoonfuls. I was in a sort of stupor. For days, I guess.

"But gradually I began to get stronger, and I asked her where I was. She wouldn't say much, except to tell me I must rest. Once or twice the two men came in. They never said anything. Occasionally at night I could hear a radio, but it was never tuned to news reports. I wondered if anyone knew where I was, or was looking for me.

"When I was able to sit up, I swung my legs over the side of the couch I was on. Then I got to my feet and keeled over in a dead faint."

"People usually do that when they've been in bed for weeks," Mary said.

"Sure," said Brillhart. "Anyway, the woman couldn't get me back on the couch, and when the men came home and found out what had happened the older one chained me—*chained* me, by God!—to the leg of the couch. I couldn't move more than a couple feet from it. The chain wasn't very heavy but in my condition it was enough.

"But an odd thing happened. The woman and I developed a sort of friendship. She never said much; she was youngish, with prematurely gray hair, and was deadly afraid of the men. One day I asked her for a razor because I could feel that I'd grown quite a beard. Presently she came back with a basin of hot water, an old-fashioned straight-edged razor and soap and a mirror. I looked in the mirror—there was two inches of beard on my face. I asked her what the date was; she shrugged that she didn't know. But after I'd shaved and tried to cut my hair a little—it took me about an hour—she whispered, 'March twenty-second.' I'd been there almost three months.

"Next day when she brought my food, which was usually pork and grits or beans, though sometimes rabbit or venison, I tried to talk to her. She put her hand on my forehead to pacify me. But it was a kind of love pat, if you know what I mean, and I began to get the message. This was the first time she was seeing me as I normally looked. She liked me."

Brillhart spoke with assurance and I studied that assurance, not being the kind of guy myself who knocks women particularly dead. I was curious about what made him attractive. Four women that I knew of (there must have been many more) had fallen for him, one had killed herself over him—and now there was this fifth one he was telling about. But Brillhart accepted them as his due.

As he gained strength over a period of days, he said, he had worked on the woman's sympathies and gradually learned from her what he needed to know. He was in a remote part of Rockland County, and these people were Jackson Whites, that strange inbred clan which has lived in the area's lonely hills, with primitive disregard for modern ways and laws since the eighteenth century.

(*The Jackson Whites are one of the great anomalies in the progress of American civilization. Their origin rests in the fact that during the late eighteenth century a man named Jackson—his first name is apparently lost to history—contracted with the English government to bring thirty-five hundred English prostitutes to this country to entertain English troops here. Some of the women were kidnapped off London streets; one ship sank en route and Jackson, who was paid by the head, replaced the fifty thus lost with West Indian women. When the English evacuated New York City during the American Revolution and went to Nova Scotia, they could not take the women, who were thus thrown on the town. Ostracized and despised, they left the city, moving north and west—starving, snapped at by dogs, hated by neighboring farmers. They finally found refuge in the wilderness of the Ramapo Mountains in northern New Jersey and southern New York State, and were soon joined by other pariahs—Tuscorara Indians cast out of North Carolina, runaway Hessians, Negro slaves, stranded Dutch, Portuguese, Spanish and Italians. They have kept to themselves since, produced some strange racial strains (including a number of albinos) and today still live a suspicious, lawless existence in poverty-stricken hovels away from everyone else. There may be as many as five thousand of them.)

But the remarkable thing was the reason why he was a prisoner.

On the morning they found him the two men—they were father and son, and the woman was the son's wife—had been hunting deer. It was out of season of course but a Jackson White observes the game laws like a southern mountaineer respects moonshining laws. They had come on a doe and her fawn in the early half-light and both fired several times. They thought they had hit one, but when they ran forward into the woods where the deer had fled, they stumbled on Brillhart. They naturally assumed they had wounded him.

The older man wanted to finish him off, but the younger was more humane and insisted they take him home. By such a slender thread had Brillhart's life been preserved, despite, as he afterward discovered, four wounds in his chest and shoulder, one of them near the heart.

The rest of the story was predictable.

"The men were away from the house almost every day, but nights they'd argue about me in low voices downstairs. They weren't sure what to do with me and I had some bad moments. The old man still favored doing away with me. I tried to tell them when I got the chance that they had not wounded me and that I knew it, and knew who had, but the old man especially was suspicious. He thought I was lying just to get away—to bring the law back on them. The younger argued they could blindfold me some night, take me somewhere miles away and dump me, and I'd never be able to find my way back. He was right too. Those were long, bad winter nights.

"The woman cleaned the blood from my clothes and occasionally washed my only shirt. You can imagine how I treated her, while I disguised how much strength I was regaining. She had hardly been away from this weird, backwoods dump all her life. She'd seen two movies in her twenty-eight years; her eyes glowed as she told me every detail of each one. I told her if she'd come to the city with me I could get her a job and she'd see movies every night. Maybe I promised her a little more than that—you know, just to make it attractive. But one day she brought me some old pliers I figured could cut through the chain in thirty minutes, with luck. And a few days later she said they were all going to a wedding celebration some seven miles away.

"I told her this was our chance. She was to start for the wedding party but pretend to be ill and return by herself. We'd have the night to escape. I held my breath while I held her red, rough hand and waited for her answer. But she finally nodded yes, and later even brought me a file that would simplify things. The next night, by the time she got back, I was free and seeing the downstairs for the first time—God, you should have seen the primitive dump! I'd made some sandwiches and took a bottle of water and we started out. I had no money—her menfolks had seen to that!—but she had a few quarters and dimes she'd stashed away over the months.

"We walked, or rather stumbled, all night. She got lost more than once, the idiot, and there was no moon. But finally we reached a sort of trail that wended downhill and I figured it would have to take us someplace. To make a long story short, we finally reached a gravel road and that took us to a highway and then—it was after daylight—a small town called Goodrich and I saw a bus sign in a store window. I parked her in a diner where we ordered coffee and I took the money and said I'd see about bus tickets. It was kind of frightening being out on a street in broad daylight after those weeks of semidarkness. Every second I expected her husband and father-in-law to pop up behind me with their guns.

"They didn't, of course, and I got a break at last. A bus for Haverstraw was due in a few minutes, and I had money enough for one ticket. I bought it and a candy bar, and got on the bus when it came in. That was the last I saw of Joanna."

"Joanna?"

"That was her name. At Haverstraw I got off—I was penniless—and thumbed a ride, I was so damned anxious to get out of that area. I gradually thumbed my way into Manhattan. When I got into town I walked to my apartment, got the caretaker to let me in and fell into bed."

"What about Joanna?" asked Archie.

"Well, what about her? She found her way there; I guess she's found her way back. I don't imagine they made her wash dishes very long for the price of two coffees."

"It was mean," said Mary indignantly.

"I think it was a dirty trick," said Archie.

I was beginning to dislike Brillhart. "I think it was stupid," I said.

That attracted his attention as mere accusations could not.

"What was stupid?" he said. "I had to get out, didn't I?"

"Sure. But you've also mentioned that you want to do something about the man who really shot you! This woman, Joanna, will be an important witness to the nature and extent of your wounds. You should have kept her a friendly witness. Now you've made sure that she hates your guts."

"Jesus!" There was anguish in his voice. "I never thought I'd need her in court."

I felt a lot better.

"As a matter of fact," I went on, and it was pure nastiness, "as a matter of fact, you really ruined your case, for now who is going to prove anything for you? The two men, the father and son, will never admit anything. The girl must hate you. Who's going to testify you were ever held a prisoner? There's only your word for a story that sounds fantastic on the face of it."

"Sure," Archie chimed in, "especially since the real guy—" he caught himself—"uh...the guy who...uh...kept you prisoner will never admit it."

Brillhart looked shrewdly at him. Brillhart was a perceptive man where his own welfare was concerned. "It seems to me," he said, "that you're eager to discourage me."

I said, "Why should anyone want to do that?"

To answer my question all he had to do was to see Archie look fearfully first at Mary, then at her brother. But her brother didn't look at Archie. He looked at me.

"Maybe," he said, "because someone is afraid of a scandal, perhaps?"

I said, "What's scandalous about being shot by an old psychopath, as you've described him? You were just the victim of circumstances. There's nothing disgraceful about that."

Brillhart's mouth pursed. He was trying to decide whether I could possibly know anything about this or whether his own guilty conscience was affecting his judgment. He decided on the latter, for after a moment he said, "You are right, of course. I've been brooding about it too long."

"That's understandable, dear," said his sister gently. "Though I still feel badly about the girl."

Brillhart didn't hear her.

"Don't think I'm not going to do something about it tomorrow," he said. "Then maybe I'll be in touch with you, Deacon. Meanwhile—this was all in confidence."

"Oh, absolutely. Not a word to anyone."

"Let me freshen your drink, Deac," said Archie, although I'd not tasted it. I said no thanks. I wanted to leave before Brillhart did and got a chance to learn I could hardly have dropped in by accident.

Waiting on the corner for a cab I reflected on how there was more than one way for a man to come back from the dead. And when I thought of what a surprise Brillhart had coming tomorrow when he tried to find Rudolf Jersey, I laughed out loud to the dark street.

# CHAPTER 2

*Two With*

Next morning I got a surprise, too.

I was deeply, happily asleep when the phone rang. It was the researcher at the office who had worked with me on resuscitation. The story was going to press this week, starting today, she told me, and added that it might be as well if I started getting in on time, at least this week. It seems it was 10:15.

I grinned and said I'd try, started some coffee, and began to shave. I had half a face yet to go when the phone rang again. This time it was Archie.

"I want to tell you how much I appreciated your standing by last night."

"I didn't do anything."

"Yes, you did. You steadied me when I was damned afraid of blurting something out."

"Archie, I'm in hell's own rush. But I want to say one thing. When I got there last night you had decided on a certain course, so naturally I played along with it. But I think you've got to change course."

"What do you mean?"

I looked at my watch. It was 10:30.

"I think you'd better tell Mary the truth. And soon. If she really loves you—and I know she does—she can't possibly hold you responsible for what you did."

"But, *Deac*!"

It was a wail of agony. "I can't possibly—quite aside from holding me responsible, you don't realize how much Mary thinks of *him*. You and I know what a heel he is. But to her he's still the spoiled, talented kid she grew up with. He's all the family she has. How can I tell her what a louse he really has made of himself?"

I said, "I've got to ring off, I'm sorry but I do. Let me remind you of one thing, though. Now that he's back Brillhart will be seeing his old friends. That includes the three girls who know that we knew about this. They don't know everything, or how much of a hand you really had in it. But we had to tell them quite a lot. Sooner or later Brillhart is going to learn that when he spun us his tale about an anonymous old psychopath attacking him for an imagined grievance, we knew whom he was talking about and what the grievance really was. Maybe you can convince him that you kept silent to protect him from embarrassment before his sister. But Brillhart is a cagey guy, and he's bound to be suspicious of how we came by this knowledge—there's the little point of not ever having gone to the police about it, you know. I think he's going to smell a conspiracy against him. That's why I think you'd be wise to tell Mary the facts before he tells her his distorted suspicions."

"But—"

"I've got to run, Archie."

I felt a little guilty handing his burden over to him like that. It was like giving a child a physical task beyond his strength. Besides, I'd grown fond of Archie and wanted him to get along with his Mary. But I had my own affairs, too. I finished shaving, gulped coffee, and hurried uptown.

Two days later the story was going to press and not well, the managing editor having taken half a page away from us, and I was rewriting in an effort to compress salient facts into half the space that they deserved. When the telephone interrupted me I growled and kept on growling.

It was Archie, of course, although he got the intimation right away.

"I'm sorry if I interrupted you in something."

"What's on your mind?"

"Well, just Brillhart."

"Yes. Will tomorrow do as well?" I looked at the half-finished piece of copy in my typewriter. Even as I did, an idea occurred to me and while Archie went on talking I typed it in with one finger.

"Sure. I guess so. It's just—well, I wanted to tell you that you were absolutely right. Brillhart smells a rat."

I finished my one-finger typing and read the sentence. It condensed a paragraph of the original. I turned back to Archie. "Brillhart? You mean he's gone to Mary?"

"No. He's—he's come to me."

I was scanning the next paragraph. If I could do that again, I'd have it almost licked.

"He's blackmailing me," Archie said.

That woke me up.

"What do you mean?"

"He suspects plenty—like you said he would. He doesn't know the truth but I don't dare tell him the truth, either. So I'm over a barrel. He got a thousand dollars from me this morning."

The researcher appeared in the doorway, looking harried. She is a pretty girl, named Madelyn, intelligent and helpful. "They're yelling for copy," she said apologetically. At that moment I hated her. I hated Archie, too.

"Be right with you," I told her.

"...And of course that's not the end," he was saying. "It isn't the money that bothers me. It's just that I hate to think of what'll happen if...Mary..."

The truth is I was shocked by what he had told me, but I did not have time to be shocked. People who have never worked against news deadlines will not be able to understand that. I said, "Look, you've paid him off. That'll keep him quiet for a day or two, anyway. Now, for Christ's sake, let me finish what I'm doing. I'll talk to you later."

"Oh, sure. It's just—have you got just one more minute?"

"No, damn it, I haven't," I said, and hung up, ashamed of myself even as I did. *"Who* is yelling for copy?" I demanded of Madelyn, though I knew very well. "We've got until five o'clock. Theoretically."

"Sure," she said. "Oh, sure. But the copy room..." She disappeared.

I turned back to the original story and what I had managed to rewrite of it. I hated the world and everyone in it.

* * * *

But next day, with the story closed tight and everything all done, I felt relieved and conscience-stricken. Relieved because the story really had turned out all right and conscience-stricken because I felt I'd been unkind to Archie. I still felt a little resentful at his demands on my time and I was damned if I was going to apologize, but after eating a late and solitary lunch, with nothing of importance to do the rest of the afternoon, I found myself in a phone booth calling Brillhart's apartment. I had an idea.

Brillhart didn't answer and neither did Eulalia, who was my next idea. Then I dialed the music publishing company and asked Don Quayle where could I reach Brillhart?

"You just missed them," he said. "Brill and Eulalia just left here."

"Know where they were going?"

"All he said was they were going to get a hamburger."

It was a long, unlikely chance but the story was done, it had come off well, and I was feeling a little tall. And I felt badly about what I'd said to Archie. A cab made it from Park Avenue to the Broadway building where Quayle's company is located in nine minutes and the next question was where you would go for a hamburger if you were leaving that building. Knowing Brillhart, I didn't think it would be Sardi's.

The third place I looked in was the right one. It was halfway down Forty-eighth Street with a counter, many bright lights in the ceiling and some tables at the back. Eulalia was at one of them, and as I sat down at the counter and ordered the coffee and Danish I didn't want, I saw Brillhart in the mirror before me step out of a telephone booth and wave to her. She got up and walked toward Brillhart, behind me. I bent over my coffee.

Brillhart gave her the receiver, they laughed together about something, then he returned to the table while she talked on the phone. I followed Brillhart to their table and a waitress followed me, bringing them two hamburgers redolent with onion slices, a bottle of chili sauce, and two coffees.

I guess I was feeling pretty tall. I said, "Hi," and stood over him a little contemptuously.

He looked up from his hamburger and said, "Hi," only half recognizing me.

I dropped down in Eulalia's chair. "I have a message."

My voice grated and he got it. He said, "Why don't you sit down?"

"You owe Archie Sinclair a thousand dollars. Get it to him by Saturday."

He put down the hamburger.

"That gives you three days."

He wasn't stupid enough to pretend indignation. But in a few words of basic English he told me what I could do.

I laughed. "Know the laws about extortion in New York State, Brillhart?"

He smiled back. "Know anything about trying to prove extortion?" he said. "Got any witnesses? Aside from my own brother-in-law? He'll never complain."

"He won't have to."

"Who will?"

"I will."

He looked a question and I answered it. "Just because I don't like you." We looked each other over. Sometimes it's nice to feel someone hating you.

"Listen, Brillhart. I know why Rudolf Jersey tried to kill you. I know what you did to his daughter. And I know how much Archie Sinclair really knows about the whole thing. Which is nothing."

"How?" He made a try for insolence. "How do *you* know about it?"

"Because Jersey told me," I lied happily, "a week before he died." I hoped I had got Archie out of trouble. "I interviewed him for a story on pop music. He was sick, I realize now—he rambled on and got talking. You know what an old man is like."

"It's your word against mine. If Arch wants to loan me a grand, that's our business. Family business. If my sister—"

"Sure," I grinned. "Your business is your business. Mine is mine. My business is news stories. Remember the story you thought you might give me—the one you were going to threaten Jersey with? Things are different now. You've discovered Jersey's dead. But the story isn't. Think of it—a heel Broadway song writer seduced the daughter of famous composer whose mysterious suicide is now finally solved. The composer tries to kill the song writer. The song writer comes back from the dead—interviews with those hillbillies here, Brillhart! We can find them, and when they learn they really never shot you they'll be glad to talk. Then for a climax we go into your blackmail attempts. What a story! Eh, Brillhart?"

It was the most colossal lie of all, for my magazine does not print stories like that. We're not a scandal sheet.

But Brillhart lived too close to the stuff of scandal to appreciate any other kind of news.

"Where'll you be, Brillhart? Your own mother won't spit on you. Maybe she won't anyway. But what'll happen to your career? What will the columnists say? Where'll you stand in the music business? Or anywhere?"

I hadn't realized I had gotten up, or was talking loud. I'd started to put on an act, but now it was genuine, and other people could hear it.

I dropped my voice. "You get that grand back to Sinclair by Saturday noon, or by Jesus you'll spend Saturday night trying to explain things in Hogan's office. Saturday's the night we go to press."

His eyes were frightened and I knew I'd won.

I left. It's the first time I ever walked out of a restaurant without remembering to pay my check.

It was two days later that Twit-Twit and I ran into the Sinclairs, quite by accident, at a movie preview. While the girls exchanged greetings, Archie pulled me aside and breathed that he had had a weird experience. Brillhart had called him the day before and said that he had meant the thousand dollars merely as a loan. Furthermore, he had brought Archie four hundred of it only a couple of hours ago, said he would have the rest early next week and strongly insisted that Archie let me know what had happened. Archie was dumbfounded.

The girls were looking at us, so I said I thought I could explain the whole thing later and that if Brillhart did not deliver as promised Archie should let me know.

I guess I felt pretty chesty. At least, I thought, *l'affaire Brillhart* was settled.

# CHAPTER 3

## *Surprise Attack*

But in the days that followed I also felt some unlikely apprehensions. I had a persistent feeling that not only had I been walking on thin ice but that I was still on it. I don't exactly know why; logically there was every reason to think that the Brillhart matter was at an end. He had nothing to gain by attracting attention to his near-murder and the shameful reason that had motivated it. The three women could still talk if they wanted, yet whom could they hurt, except themselves and perhaps Brillhart? Not Jersey, certainly. Not me. And not Archie. No one but Archie and myself knew of his ex post facto participation in the attempted murder of Brillhart. And in any case Brillhart was alive.

Yet I felt uneasy.

It was like being in an empty room and hearing whispers behind you, whispers that could not come from any known source and yet were audible. It was the quick blur of movement you glimpse at a dark window at midnight, the flicker that makes you look a second time and which you never really see. It was the feeling that things are happening and events are in train, and you don't know what they are.

You only sense them.

And even then you are not sure. Just uneasy.

* * * *

Inez Low came to see me at the office on a gloomy morning of steady rain that I remember because it was my birthday. We had just finished a story conference and I was leafing through the mail when my phone rang and the lobby receptionist said Miss Low was here. I said Mr. Deacon would see Miss Low. A few minutes later Inez stood in the doorway, her transparent plastic raincoat glistening with rain, her face bright with fresh make-up and an expectant smile. I hung up the raincoat, she exuded a dry, unfamiliar perfume, and looked chic in a cream-colored suit. She obviously had fixed herself up for someone; I wondered whether it was for me or a lunch date.

She said it was nice to see me, sat down, and let me light her cigarette. She smiled her thanks but it was a mechanical smile and I recognized that behind these conventions there lay a serious purpose.

What was on her mind came out right away. "Seen Brill lately?"

"Not for some time."

"Mind telling me when you last saw him?"

"Not at all. It must have been up at his sister's, several weeks ago."

"You haven't seen him since?"

"What's this all about, if you don't mind telling me?"

She put the cigarette to wet-paint lips and drew long on it. As she did, her face lost the beauty it still possessed and became calculating and old.

"Brill's missing," she said. "No one's seen him for a week."

I laughed. "Are we doing the 'I had a date with him last night' bit again? Or do you want to tell me he left his pipe at your apartment?"

"I'm serious."

"So am I."

She ground out her cigarette deliberately in the ashtray on my desk. She said, "Now, look," just as deliberately, "What I'm telling you is that he has *disappeared.* No one has seen him. And what I want to know is what you know about it."

"That's nothing," I said. "Why should I? He and I weren't friends."

"Or enemies?"

"Don't be silly."

"Why do you have a key to his apartment?"

"I don't."

"You did."

"I don't now."

"Look, Mr. Deacon." She took out another cigarette. I lighted that one, too.

"I didn't come here to start a row. Some time back you impressed me the way you figured out that gag the girls and I arranged. Now it's no gag— Brill's really missing and I was sort of hoping I could interest you in doing something about it. There might even be a story in it for your magazine." Again the calculating stare.

I don't know why people are always trying to tell you what might be a story for your magazine. I don't go around telling night club singers how to belt "After You've Gone."

"Sorry. I doubt if anything has happened to Brillhart, especially like the last time. After all, he's fairly footloose. Maybe he just went out of town for a while."

"You mean with a girl."

"That's not what I said. It's a possibility. But there are lots of others. And I can tell you this. None of them add up to a magazine story. I don't think many people give a damn what might happen to Brillhart."

"Look, Mr. Deacon, I'm going to level with you. I don't really give a"— she used a word—"what happened to him. But here's the thing. He owes me money and I need it. Furthermore, if anything's happened to him, I'm still his widow and I inherit. That's my interest. Furthermore, I can tell you this. When he came back from—from that little adventure up in Rockland County he called me and told me he was going to have a lot of money soon. He said I didn't have to worry about what he owed me—I'd soon get it. He sounded happy and—you know. Prosperous."

"How much does he owe you?"

She paused. "Just under sixteen thousand."

Brillhart had really planned to take Rudolf Jersey. "That's a fair sum."

"I made good money in my time, honey."

"Frankly I think you've got nothing to worry about. Brill will turn up, and if he's so confident and prosperous—"

"He isn't any more." The second cigarette, half smoked, was ground out and she began fumbling through her purse for number three.

"How do you know about him, if he's missing?"

"Maybe I'd better tell you all of it."

"Maybe."

"It began over two weeks ago." We collaborated on lighting a third cigarette. "Brill was having a hamburger with Eulalia Pope—he was happy as a lark. He'd connected with some dough. They talked of marriage. She says he was buoyant.

"Well, they were thinking of visiting friends up in Fairfield County for the weekend and first Brill talked to them on the phone, then Eulalia did. When Brill went back to the table, while Eulalia talked, a man came up and he and Brill spoke. When Eulalia got back to the table Brill was a changed guy. He was down, he was gloomy and grim. She said the weekend was all set and Brill said forget it. He couldn't make it. He didn't have a nickel. And Eulalia says he looked—well, scared."

I tried to remember whether the phone booth had been visible from the table. I had looked once to see if Eulalia was coming out, and I clearly recalled that I couldn't see the phone booth at all. So all I said was, "Is that so?"

"Yes. That's how it began. About a week later he disappeared."

"How did he do that?"

"How the hell do I know? That's the point. The last person to see him, far as I can learn, was the caretaker of his apartment. That was eight days ago—he saw Brill leaving in the morning. No one's seen him since."

"Frankly, Miss Low, I think he'll turn up. In any case there's nothing I can do about it. There's no story in this, and I'm not equipped to do a missing persons hunt."

She ground out the third cigarette. The ashtray was getting a little full. She said, "There's one thing."

"What's that?"

"You can answer a question. An honest question. And I want an honest answer."

"Go ahead. Let's be honest."

"Okay. Mr. Deacon, was it you who talked to Brill that day while Eulalia was in the phone booth?"

"Me?"

"Because Eulalia thinks it was you. She came out of the phone booth as the man was leaving, so she only glimpsed him. But later she thought his back looked a little like yours."

"She's insane."

"Maybe. But the fact remains Brill hated you—that's for sure."

*"Me?"* I hoped it sounded surprised. "Why do you say that?"

"He came up to see me a little over a week ago. Just before he—he turned up missing. He was a little drunk and he tried to tap me for fifty bucks. Before he got through he was begging for even a five. But he said one of these days he was going to get you good. He was drunk, of course."

"He didn't say why he wanted to get me?"

"No. But when I told Eulalia about it she put two and two together and figured you might have been the guy in the restaurant."

"God, what people like you two can come up with! It's a good thing it takes more than that to get a conviction in court."

"Well, don't hold me responsible. I didn't put any stock in her ideas from the beginning. As a matter of fact, when Brill talked about you, he was sort of drunk, as I said, and he soon went into something else—a new business deal he had in mind that he said would make the other one look like peanuts."

"What deal was that?"

"He didn't say. But he hinted I would get something out of it, too, and that he wanted me to. He made that plain. And I don't think it was the drinks." She sounded oddly tender about a man she hated.

"I'm sure he meant it," I said tactfully.

"But I wish you would do something about finding him, or tell me what to do. Should I go to the police?"

He had hinted he might have some money for her, and now he's missing, so she's anxious about him, I thought. Of course, I have a cynical mind. I said:

"Do as you think best. You're still his wife. But I don't think you need the police. I think he'll show up, someplace or other."

And I was right.

I'm not boasting about it.

\* \* \* \*

It was still raining when I left the office that night a little after six. It had rained all day, with a monotonous insistence that suggested it would go on forever. I wasn't consciously thinking about it. Inez's visit had had a vaguely threatening note which didn't exactly worry me and yet had made me wonder through the afternoon what might happen if she continued to go around talking to people. And the rain had continued. And it was my birthday.

At the building entrance there were a few people waiting for taxis and one of them was Charlie Kavanagh, another staff member. Apparently he had been there first because when a cab pulled up Charlie got it and, looking around, saw me.

"You going downtown?" he said, and I nodded and got in.

Charlie said that it was a lousy night, the traffic was impossible, and the magazine sure needed a shot in the arm. I agreed because it was his cab and he had not had a story in the magazine for some time.

When we had crossed Fourteenth Street I asked Charlie to have a drink with me. He said no, because his wife was waiting for him, and I got out at Twelfth Street and thought how nice it must be to have a wife to be getting home to on a night like this. I have reached the age where you no longer get sentimental about birthdays, but I am not so old I cannot remember other ones, when there were people who knew when you were born and recalled it with cakes and bright candles and even gave you presents.

This was just a rainy night on lower Fifth Avenue. But I decided that on my birthday I owed myself a drink, so I went into the Grosvenor and had a Martini and it was good enough so that I ordered a second.

"Merry Christmas," I told myself, "Happy New Year," and something of Masefield's crossed my mind, a poem that begins:

When I am buried, all my thoughts and acts
Will be reduced to lists of dates and facts...
And none will know the gleam there used to be
About the feast days freshly kept by me...

I sipped the second Martini and considered what I most wanted to do after a little light supper; call someone, or try for a single theater ticket, or discover there was something worth watching on television, or begin a new book? Maybe I should start *War and Peace,* I thought. I have never read *War and Peace.* What better night to start *War and Peace* than on your birthday?

Maybe by my next birthday, I'll have finished it, I thought.

I unfurled my paper, and looked at the top half of the *Journal's* front page. There was a picture there. It was Brillhart's.

It was the same picture I'd seen at Kim Winter's. Now it was three columns wide, and above it was a four-column head, over a story that began:

Orman "Brill" Brillhart, 43-year-old composer of many song hits, has been found murdered in the wilds of Rockland County, Sheriff Mel Boyd announced today.

I didn't exactly believe what I was reading. For a long moment I didn't *feel* anything. It was just so much type on a page that delivered a message as remote as a star gleam. Besides, I had been through this before and it had all been wrong. Yet now, intuitively, I knew that this wasn't another fantasy. This time Brillhart had got it. And the story, when my eyes found it again, confirmed my intuition.

Brillhart, who authored such hits as "I'll Always Be Around" and "Waiting for the Waiter," was found in a lonely ravine six miles from Cold Springs. He had been shot four times in the chest.

Sheriff Boyd said a medical examination indicated the song writer had been dead for at least a week. He was dressed in ordinary clothes and had been shot at close range. No clues as to the motive or killer were immediately apparent, authorities indicated.

Brillhart was discovered by surveyors making a study of a new throughway entrance.

I put the paper on the bar, thought about what this might do to Archie, and Eulalia, and Inez (her question was answered!), and Kim. I slowly finished my drink, paid, tipped, and left.

As I did, I thought of the quarrel I had had with Brillhart, and how, even with the best of intentions, I had intruded on his life. I reminded myself what hell is paved with.

It is strange what involvement with a dead man, however innocent, can do to your equilibrium. A shapeless, nameless worry began growing within me, in the way that a major storm forms up.

It was in this mood that I walked to my apartment, let myself in, and mounted the flight of stairs. There is one thing wrong with my apartment. It is in an old, reconstructed brownstone on Twelfth Street and the light switch is across the foyer. If it is night, you walk in through darkness and fumble for the switch.

I walked in and fumbled for the switch.

Someone grabbed my arms. Someone else grabbed my knees and a big, heavy cloth like a blanket went over my head. I was forced down before I knew what was happening and then bent over on my knees, head down. I tried to fight back but it didn't work because whoever was holding my arms was big and knew what he was doing. Crazily, I thought of Brillhart. But Brillhart was dead.

I tried to kick backwards a couple of times but you can't on your knees. Then there was a click and out of a corner of the blanket over my head I saw a gleam of light. "Let him up," a man said.

I got to my feet.

They kept the blanket pulled down over me, and an odd voice, half male and half female, said, "Why don't we kill him here?" and another voice, a girl's but disguised, said, "Naw. Out by the reservoir."

"No," said the man. "The brickyard."

"In any case," the girl said, "no knives. We'll drown him in Martinis."

I caught a little of a familiar scent then. "Don't do this terrible thing!" I whimpered. "Don't make me suffer. If you're going to kill me, do it fast."

I was pushed forward and the blanket was whisked off my head. In front of me was the small table where I eat dinner when I'm alone. On it were some new records, a magnum of champagne, a shaker of Martinis, a large crock of caviar and small ones of chopped onion and egg. There was also a first edition of *The Hound of the Baskervilles* and a couple of ties.

I didn't have to look around to see who was behind me.

"Thanks," I said after a minute. "Thanks, you fatheads."

It was a birthday after all. Twit-Twit and Betsy kissed me and Dolan poured champagne. I forgot about Brillhart.

# CHAPTER 4

*What Cohen Knew*

At 11:45 that evening we were all sitting around the table, in what might be called a state of congenial crowdedness (my dining space is not very big) and convivial happiness (Tom was hating champagne as much as usual). My hosts, since I can hardly call them guests, had brought along some *pate,* two cooked ducks *a l'orange,* and some Chablis for me. There had been Martinis first, and everyone was fairly relaxed. Now we sat over coffee and the remnants of a birthday cake, and they debated amiably where I should be taken to complete the celebration. Twit-Twit mentioned the Persian Room because she was in a new dress; I forgot to say that the women had even dressed semi-formally for the occasion. But Betsy said we should go to Condon's because I liked it there.

While the girls debated the matter, Tom turned his gaze to the front of Twit-Twit's dress. It was sort of off the shoulder, but it was also off other things. The result was something to catch the eye of any red-blooded boy.

There was a moment's silence and Tom said, "If there's anything I like, it's a room with a view." His gaze stayed where it was. Twit-Twit gave him her crinkly smile.

"I love the rolling hills," Tom went on.

"Not to mention the purple valleys," I said.

"Exactly," said Tom. "Let us not forget the purple valleys. And finally, and most of all, there are the bosky dells."

Everyone laughed, Twit-Twit as much as anyone, but I noticed she was blushing. She got up.

"One brandy float all around and we take off for somewhere," she said. "No, sit down, Deac. This is your birthday. You can't work tonight." She went into the kitchen but I followed her. As I did, I heard Tom say, "What's wrong with the bosky dells?"

"It is a nice dress," I said. "On a nice girl."

"I guess I don't do badly for a girl who takes a B-cup." She was floating brandy in a glass. "Don't jiggle me, idiot." I kept my arms around her.

"Old mother Twickenham," I said in her ear. "Stirring up another batch of pineapple upside-down cake."

She stopped pouring cognac.

"I remember it so well," I said. "The old-fashioned kitchen, redolent of gingerbread and pig's knuckles."

"And sauerkraut."

"Of course." I kissed her. It was a hell of a practical dress.

After a minute, I said, "Thanks for the party."

After another minute she said, "I must pour brandy." When we went back into the living room Tom was on his feet, prowling. He had put a record on the hi-fi and Sidney Bechet's "One O'Clock Jump" was moving along wonderfully.

"We've been trying to figure out where to take you," he said. "I mentioned the S.P.C.A."

"But we haven't paid last month's bill there," said Betsy. "Tom brought them three agency men for extermination last month. That runs into money."

"I can imagine."

"This gets us nowhere," said Tom. He switched off the sound. "Let's be serious. Where do we go? Where's that brandy? Thanks, Twit-Twit." He put it away, then frowned at the carpet. "Where to?" He began whistling through his teeth.

"Oh, God," said Betsy. "He's whistling 'The Blues in the Night.' You don't know what it means when Dolan starts whistling 'The Blues in the Night.' The last time he did it we wound up in this dump down on First Avenue."

"That's it," cried Tom. He snapped his fingers. "That's where we go. That Pope dame is singing there—we're thinking of signing her for the week after next."

"Eulalia Pope?"

"That's the one. I'd like to hear her, just to know what we're buying."

"Isn't that the one who's a friend of Brillhart's?" Twit-Twit said.

Tom looked at her in surprise. "That's right. Her brother called me today and told me how anxious she was to work. Then she got on the phone, and gave me the same pitch. You know why? She said she needed money to hire a private detective to find Brillhart."

"She can save her money," I said.

"What do you mean?"

"His body was found up in Rockland County today. Brillhart's dead."

"Not again!" said Twit-Twit.

"He's dead," I said.

"There won't be a wet eye in the house," said Tom.

I told them what details I'd read in the final edition.

"Well, well," Tom said. "Imagine that! He's dead. Well, well. Do we go hear Eulalia?"

That was Brillhart's obituary notice.

"Why not?" Twit-Twit sacrificed her dress.

The doorbell rang.

Going to the foyer, I thought, it's 12:15. If this is something from the office like an assignment, I am not going to be here. I'm out, that's all. This is too good an evening.

It wasn't the office.

"Mr. Deacon?" The voice was smooth and polite, considering it came from the usually squawky vestibule phone.

"Yes."

"Awfully sorry to disturb you so late. This is Lieutenant Cohen of the Police Department. Could I come up for a moment?"

I felt things sink inside of me. "Sure," I said.

* * * *

Lieutenant Hyman Cohen was a slight man with black curly hair and black-button eyes, who moved gracefully. His suit of Glenurquhart plaid looked as if it had been draped in Bond Street, and the pale blue shirt was becoming to his olive complexion. I have spent a lot of time with policemen and I know they do not have big feet, or chew cigars, or keep their hats on. Even so, Cohen looked less like a cop than any I have ever met. He looked stylish and sophisticated, and he made me nervous.

I took his raincoat and immaculate snap-brim hat, led him past the living-room door into the bedroom and closed the door.

"I can't tell you how I regret breaking in like this," he said. "Especially when I gather you have guests."

"Not at all. Maybe I could offer you a drink."

"Not while I'm working." He sighed and leaned back, extending perfectly stained brogues. "You have one."

"Not if you won't."

"You think I'm being official?"

"It'd be less official if you had a drink."

"Then I will. You forced me." He grinned. "Scotch and water."

I got two drinks, told the others a little tensely who my visitor was, and closed the door again.

"If you've seen the papers tonight, you probably know, why I'm here."

"Brillhart."

"Then you know the circumstances." He was gentle, well-mannered, and shot from the hip.

"Why would I?"

"Good Scotch," he murmured and quoted, "'It ascends me into the brain...' No, all I meant was that I supposed the papers carried the details. I've not had a chance to read them myself."

*I'll bet.*

"The story I read was brief. But it does arouse my curiosity."

"In what way?"

"I think it said Brillhart was found well out in Rockland County. Why would it be in the New York department's jurisdiction?"

"Because there is reason to believe"—he spoke rather lazily—"that he was killed in New York City. You see, he was found this morning between eight and eight-thirty in a field six miles west of Cold Springs by some surveyors. He was lying on his face, fully clothed, had been dragged from the road, and no effort had been made to conceal or cover the body. The face was badly scratched. He'd probably been dead about six, maybe seven, days but that's a rough estimate, pending the autopsy report. He had been shot four times in and around the heart, with a .38 caliber revolver. One of the wounds almost coincided with one of several inflicted on him some months earlier by Rudolf Jersey, also with a .38." He opened his half-closed eyes. "As you know," he said.

I said nothing.

"It is a rural area, the nearest house some three quarters of a mile away. There are no witnesses so far. But you appreciate the irony of all this. I know you are familiar with the earlier story. Rudolf Jersey tried to kill Brillhart and failed. Now someone else succeeded, apparently by simulating the earlier method. And it may have been a woman."

"A *woman*?"

"A woman called the New York police that night—April 21—at 11:50. She sounded agitated. She said a man had just been murdered and was lying in a field along Route 101 west of Cold Springs. She said he had been shot around nine o'clock and that we should go out."

"And so?"

"Cold Springs is a long way out of our jurisdiction. Our switchboard relayed the information to the local police up there. They made a routine check but found nothing. Considering the time of night and the length of road involved, you can hardly blame them for not finding a body off in a field. Besides, all police departments get a lot of crackpot calls."

"Sure. But I'm curious who told you the name of Brillhart's earlier attacker. Have you been talking to his wife?"

Cohen grinned nonchalantly. "His estranged wife, yes. Also Miss Pope. They both seem familiar with the story."

"I guess so." Thus far Archie sounded safe. "Is that drink strong? Or too weak?"

"Perfect, thanks. I gather Brillhart and Eulalia Pope were—ah, quite friendly?"

"I guess that's so."

"But there was no bitterness between him and his wife, or estranged wife, to be exact."

After a second of surprise I said, "Inez? I guess not," but I hadn't said it soon enough.

"You think there was?"

"I really wouldn't know," and recognized that I sounded like a parrot.

Cohen moved fast. "Miss Low told me she had recently been friendly with her husband, and I gathered generally it was a friendly separation. She said they had even been talking of some mutual business deal he had in mind."

"What kind of deal?"

"She said it was a sort of voice training school. Coaching, she called it. Sort of a Mr. and Mrs. Arthur Murray for voice students."

"I hadn't heard of it."

"Mr. Deacon, do you mind if I ask a few questions about your relationship with Brillhart?"

"Fire away."

"You were friends?"

"Hardly. I'd met him a few times."

"I was under the impression you visited him occasionally at his apartment."

"I've never visited Brillhart at his apartment." It wasn't really a lie, and maybe he did not know about the key.

"When did you last see him?"

Now it was time for truth. Maybe Eulalia had not recognized me for sure, but she'd have mentioned me to Cohen. And someone else might have seen me.

"In a hamburger restaurant on Forty-eighth Street about two weeks ago. Near Broadway."

"Then it *was* you."

"Yes."

He waited. Then, "I gather you talked. Want to tell me what you talked about?"

"Not especially. I talked tough to him. Like someone who—who might do him some damage."

"Why?"

"Brillhart was threatening to break up a marriage. A happy marriage."

"Whose?"

It was either me or Archie. I decided that for a while at least it would be me.

"I won't go into that."

"Why not, Mr. Deacon?" Gently. Almost hurt.

"Because to tell you might accomplish just what Brillhart was threatening to do."

"Don't you think I can keep a secret?"

"I do indeed. But you are in an official position. Depending on what turns this thing may take, you could have to report what I tell you to others. I can't take that responsibility."

"Even if I were to promise—"

"If you were to promise me something, I'd believe you because I am sure you keep promises. But you are not in a position to make promises at this stage. Are you?"

He looked sadder.

"I'll tell you this much. I threatened Brillhart with exposure in a magazine story that would have made him out a prize heel. It was an absurd threat because my magazine would never publish such a story. But, you see, Brillhart had a guilty conscience—he *was* a heel! So it never occurred to him to question what I threatened."

He was looking down at his hands.

"I wanted to bluff him and, as I happen to know, I succeeded. I did not threaten to kill him, believe it or not. Incidentally, I did not kill him."

He looked up. "Incidentally, I believe you."

"Thanks."

"Do you happen to know a Mr. Pollock, who was a friend of Brillhart's?"

He wasn't giving me much time to make decisions. "I don't know anyone of that name," I said truthfully.

"Apparently he owed Brillhart money. It has occurred to us that Brillhart might have been blackmailing him. And that Pollock could have turned on his blackmailer."

"I suppose that's possible."

"Pollock came to Brillhart's apartment one day and tried to find him, mentioning the debt to the caretaker. About the same time an attractive blonde showed up looking for Brillhart, and evidently tried to get into his apartment. There seemed no connection at the moment but now it appears the blonde might have been a blackmail victim. Or they may have been working together."

"For what purpose?" Above my own voice I heard the trill of Twit-Twit's laugh in the next room.

"Your guess is as good as mine. But we sure want to talk to Pollock and the girl. If you get any ideas—"

"I'll notify you."

He said, "One of my associates talked to Brillhart's sister—a Mrs. Archie Sinclair."

"I've met her."

"She said you were at their home when Brillhart told the story of how Mr. Jersey tried to kill him."

"That's right. But Brillhart did not mention Jersey's name. He hoped to blackmail him—at that point he didn't know Jersey was dead."

"I see." He put palms to cheeks and rubbed them slowly downward. "Busy man, Brillhart," he said.

"Very busy."

"One thing Mrs. Sinclair was not too clear on was why Brillhart happened to stay so long in the Rockland County hills without getting word to friends."

So I told him the full story of Brillhart's imprisonment and how he had betrayed the girl who helped him escape. Cohen's lips pursed as he listened and he took out his notebook and wrote some notes. From which I gathered this was the first thing I had told him that he did not already know. He said, "He didn't mention the name of this family that held him prisoner?"

"The only name he mentioned was that of the girl—Joanna. He had no idea where the house was."

"It's not much but it's a start. I guess her folks had reason enough to—to wish him ill."

"I expect they wished Brillhart quite a lot of ill."

He got up. "Thanks, Mr. Deacon. And, again, my apologies for intruding. Ah...you could do us an enormous favor if you would just let us know, in case you have to go out of town, just where you will be. There might be some point that you alone could clear up..."

Holding his raincoat for him, I smiled wryly. You talk of people being smooth as silk, but beside Cohen silk was raw burlap.

"Oh, just to straighten me out, Mr. Deacon. I gather you have never visited Brillhart's apartment."

"I didn't say that."

He turned around. "No, you didn't, did you?"

"I went up to his apartment once or twice when he was missing, and was reported being seen around town."

"Why were you interested?"

"Curiosity. I had been working on a story on resuscitation—that's trying to bring dead persons back to life."

"I know what resuscitation is."

"When I heard about Brillhart being seen around, I got curious."

"I see." He held out a hand. "I'll look forward to reading it."

"It ran in last week's magazine. I'll send you one. And maybe you wouldn't mind answering a question yourself."

"By all means."

"I gather that this time Brillhart was killed—really killed—in the same way he almost was before. Right?"

"Right—just about."

"What do you mean, just about?"

Cohen said, "The wounds were a little different, that's all. And he was found much nearer the highway than, I gather, he was found before."

I waited.

"The four bullet wounds entered his chest"—Cohen stood up and pointed his right forefinger, pistol-wise, toward his heart at the black knit necktie—"transversely, at approximately the breastbone, penetrated the heart for the most part, and exited from under the left shoulder blade."

I said, "Then he was shot from the side, and not by someone standing over him, firing directly into his heart."

"Well, the shots were fired at close range, all right. But a man can turn away pretty fast when someone pulls a gun on him and starts firing."

"Sure. But then the course of each slug is different, because he's turning while the gun is in a constant position. Did these bullets go in at different angles, or were they more or less parallel? Or do you know?"

Cohen looked at me thoughtfully. "More or less parallel."

"I see." I opened the front door for him.

"Thanks again," he said. "You *will* phone us if you have to leave New York?"

"Of course." I wondered if I was going to be tailed. I said, "One thing which is none of my business."

"Of course."

"Were you always a cop?"

The tired, dark face smiled understanding. "No. I started out in life hoping to be a rabbi. After three years of study I decided I could do more good teaching. So I taught English for four years in Bronx high schools. Tough ones."

"That's quite a jump."

"Yes. Then when I saw what some kids were up against, and how their lives were being mutilated, it seemed to me police work offered the most immediate opportunity for bettering man's lot. So I became a policeman. I hoped to do juvenile work, but instead I got sidetracked into homicide work."

Some sidetrack. "And you like it?"

"Oh, yes. Though I still hope to get back to juveniles. Good night, Mr. Deacon."

"Good night, Lieutenant Cohen."

"Mister," he corrected softly.

Back in the bedroom I picked up the drink I had not touched. I noticed he had hardly touched his.

I'd see him again.

\* \* \* \*

When I got into the office the next day, or rather the same day, it was a quarter after twelve and I got quite a reception

Where had I been? Who did I think I was? They'd called me at 10:30 (I mustn't have heard the phone), at 11:00 (in the shower), and at 11:30 (out for breakfast). Anyway, after months of stalling, the Defense Department had finally cleared me for a story involving a missiles plant in California on which I would work with a photographer, we had places on a one-o'clock plane and if I left at once I might make it. The photographer had already left. Here was $500 traveling money. Get going.

It took it. I made it.

But not until the wheels had lifted perhaps thirty feet above Idlewild's concrete did I remember that I was not to leave town without notifying Cohen.

# THE FINAL TRACES

"I am afraid, my dear Watson, that most of your conclusions were erroneous. When I said that you stimulated me I meant, to be frank, that in noting your fallacies I was occasionally guided towards the truth."

—Conan Doyle: *The Hound of the Baskervilles*

# CHAPTER 1

*Step One, Step Two*

As we flew to San Francisco I debated wiring Cohen.

Finally I thought, the hell with it. As far as Brillhart was concerned, I was innocent of any wrongdoing. If he really had to, Cohen could reach me through the office. Besides, I had a hangover, and I faced living and working for some days in one suit, without even an extra shirt, and I had had no chance to brief myself properly on the story.

Maybe that's how a story should begin—in disaster. For this one ended in triumph. Four nights later I was flying back to New York, laden with notes for a good piece. We had some excellent pictures to illustrate it and I'd even had a chance to buy some shirts and get my suit pressed.

I called Twit-Twit from the airport, waking her up, and told her she was having dinner with me that night. With surprising docility she agreed that she was. I checked in briefly at the office, told them I'd be home writing for the next several days, then went home and slept. At eight o'clock that night we were sitting across from each other in La Cloche d'Or, over hors d'oeuvres and the second Martini, with Twit-Twit looking kind of glowingly wonderful, not only to me but to some of the men at the other tables, apparently.

She said, "So you did a story involving missiles. Missiles bore me. What about this Brillhart business?"

"I've forgotten him."

She looked at me. "Have you?"

"Why not?"

"I thought that was your cup of tea. In fact, I'd expected to be dazzled by brilliant deductions tonight."

"So that's why you wanted to have dinner with me. I'd wondered."

When she is hit Twit-Twit shows it. "That isn't true. I wanted to have dinner with you because you've been away."

"I'm back."

"And that's enough." Suddenly she squeezed my hand, and suddenly I believed her because she is basically honest. This makes her very dangerous.

I said, "So what do you want to know? What is bothering you?"

"Questions. Questions like why was Brillhart killed in exactly the way someone else earlier tried to kill him—and failed. I gather from what you've told me it could not have been a case of the earlier person succeeding a second time."

"It couldn't," I said shortly. "Jersey's dead."

"Then?"

I sipped the cold, clean, lemon-tinctured Martini. "I haven't had time to think about it in the last few days. But I'd come to some conclusions earlier."

"Go on. Call me Watson, if you like."

"Lay off."

"Okay. But go on. I'm curious. Remember, this is the only reason I'm having dinner with you."

"Go to hell, you blonde witch. First tell me what's been in the papers."

"Nothing but clichés. The investigation is continuing. Leads are being run down. The autopsy showed that he was hit by four bullets and killed by three, fired fairly straight into the heart. The gun was a .36."

"That's your dress size. The gun was a .38."

"All right. Anyway, he'd been dead about a week when found. The funeral was yesterday. Private. Attended only by close friends."

"That must have made it very private."

I thought for a moment about leads being run down and what Cohen had said about Pollock and the mysterious blonde. "As a matter of fact, you're right. I ought to be more interested in Brillhart, for personal reasons."

"What personal reasons?"

I wasn't going to worry her about it.

"Only that I know a few things the police don't, and I am concerned that some innocent person doesn't get involved."

"Innocent people are usually protected by their own innocence."

Are they, my slender, blue-eyed goddess? If a certain caretaker spots you in the street someday—

She said, "You know what I think? I think the solution probably turns on living rooms."

"Don't start being enigmatic."

"I'm not. But that Brillhart should have been almost murdered once, and then actually murdered a second time—each time in the same way—is an impossible coincidence. It couldn't have just happened. I think the murder was done by someone who knew in a detailed way of the earlier attempt and then deliberately simulated it."

"What's that to do with living rooms?" I asked, and finished my hors d'oeuvres. The mussel and the last of the Martini made a fine combination.

"Living rooms are not the whole and only key. But they're a vital consideration. Look! According to what you told me, Rudolf Jersey tried to kill Brillhart—thought he had, in fact—by a certain method. It consisted of two steps, one premeditated, the other accidental. First, he carefully lured Brillhart up to his apartment and shot him. Step one. But Jersey never planned on getting away with it. So the second step—the possibility of sneaking the corpse out of his apartment and dumping it in Rockland County—was a spur-of-the-moment matter that happened to work by luck.

"But now Brillhart has really been murdered, and this time no mistake. Can it be coincidence that he was again shot with a thirty-eight? That the wounds were again multiple and again in the same place? That he was dragged up all the way to a remote part of Rockland County, especially when Manhattan is surrounded by rivers and there are so many docks and bridges from which to drop a body? Not to mention the many parks where it could be left? Indeed, is it coincidence that Brillhart was *shot* again—when guns are so noisy, and New York City so full of people, and when there are many more quiet ways of killing?"

"Those are very suggestive points."

Her eyes were like stars. "That's why living rooms are important. Someone knew what Jersey had done. Someone was familiar with both his first step, and his second. Someone recognized the whole thing as a foolproof and convenient murder pattern—if the risks which Jersey ran, or was lucky about, could be eliminated." She was very excited about it.

Henri put painfully hot plates bearing delicately broiled *sole amandine* before us and gave the wine a spin in its bucket. When he had left, Twit-Twit lowered her voice and said, "If my duplication theory is right, Brillhart was killed by someone who could easily lure him to his home and knew that no one would hear the shots there. The whole modus operandi suggests someone who had been wronged by Brillhart and who reasoned with poetic justice: Jersey tried and failed, so I'll use the same method and make it work."

Her small mouth tested the sole's temperature and found it safe. I poured wine.

"And furthermore," she said after a moment, "There are such things as silencers." That I had to answer.

"Silencers are lovely in fiction but actually they are rare. They're illegal and, while the professional criminal comes up with one occasionally, all the people we are concerned with, as far as I can see, are fairly respectable and would have trouble obtaining one. Furthermore, the thirty-eight would have to be especially sealed for the silencer to work well. It's more likely Brillhart was killed with a regular gun by someone who just started pulling the trigger, as Jersey did, and didn't stop till the gun was empty."

"Never mind—finish your dinner! We've got to start investigating living rooms. Tonight."

I laughed. "Sit back and relax. How many living rooms are involved, do you suppose?"

"How many?"

"How many people know the story of Rudolf Jersey's murder attempt? Quite a few that we know of. But Brillhart could have told many more than we know. And anyway, there's Kim Winter—I can tell you her twenty-fourth-floor duplex is big and remote enough to qualify. There's Eulalia—"

"I thought she was in love with Brillhart."

"She was. But Brillhart was a guy who could turn feminine love into hate pretty fast, if you recall. That's one reason why I'm not thinking about motive too much at the moment. If I were, I'd sure think about his ex-wife."

"Inez? What about her living room?"

"I don't know."

"And Eulalia's?"

"I don't know about either. Inez lives in a brownstone on West Seventy-first Street. Eulalia is in an apartment hotel on East Thirty-sixth. I think that last would be a tough place to fire a gun in without attracting attention. But speaking of motive, don't forget those Jackson Whites. They had good reason to hate Brillhart."

"They could hardly have known about Jersey's method."

"As a matter of fact they did." I poured what was left of the wine and the waiter took our plates. "That night at Archie's Brillhart said he had told them what had really happened, in an effort to persuade them that they were not guilty and he held no rancor. However they'd hardly leave the body in their own back yard, so to speak."

"Yes." She brooded over the *filtre* that a waiter had brought her. "Unless they wanted to advertise to their own little world that the insult to one of their women had been avenged."

"Yes." I was brooding too. "There are other possibilities."

"Such as?"

"I don't know. All I know is that Jersey is dead and that we have only Archie's word for what happened between Brillhart and Jersey."

Now her eyes were more green than blue. "That would involve Mary," she breathed.

"Not necessarily."

"Mary I refuse to accept as a suspect. She's too sweet."

"But their apartment fits the prescription."

And there was Archie's enormous high-fidelity system.

I thought of a man with a musician's sense of timing firing a pistol to recorded cymbal crashes and crescendos, one of the moderns.

I said, "Finally, there's one other suspect."

"Who's that?"

"A desperate man. Me."

"Don't be silly."

"I'm not. Sergeant Cohen isn't silly either. And he knows I had a public quarrel with Brillhart."

It wasn't a comfortable thought but it was worth it to see the troubled look come over her face. She said, "Let's get out of here."

"A cognac, Watson?"

"We've work to do."

"What work?"

"We're going to drop in on Inez and Eulalia and inspect their apartments as possible shooting galleries."

"*Now?*"

"Now, my wide-eyed boy. Tonight. Get the check."

* * * *

Eulalia's phone did not answer, which perhaps was just as well, and there was none listed for an Inez Low. So we took a cab to Seventy-first and Broadway and walked from there. That pleased Twit-Twit; she wanted the mounting excitement of the chase, even if it would be futile, rather than disappointment by telephone.

A street light in front of the brownstone where Inez lived made bizarre shadow patterns about its tall windows, like dark circles around blind eyes. The windows themselves were black, save for one in the basement and one on the third floor. The mailboxes indicated there were eight apartments—two to a floor, presumably. Inez Low lived in 3-A. The front door was not locked.

Twit-Twit pointed to Inez's button but I shook my head. Three-A should be on the second floor above the basement, according to my painfully simple deductions, and that floor was wholly dark though a window was open. Probably she was out. We walked in and climbed the half-lit stairway.

I was right. A door at the front on the third floor bore a card: Inez Low. I listened. There was no sound from within, and we had made little walking down the hall. It was unlikely that she would leave the place unlocked but you never could tell. My hand went out to try the knob.

The silence was broken by an unnerving sound. The sound of a woman sobbing in the night.

It came from the other side of the door, and apparently she was trying to control her sobs but without success, for she gasped and strangled, the outbursts dying away into a piteous weeping and then breaking out again.

We listened, reluctant and spellbound.

I pulled Twit-Twit close to me. "This is not the night to call."

She nodded, grave and wondering, and we tiptoed back down the way we had come.

I led the way across the silent street and, standing just outside the street light's circle of illumination, studied the shadowy, now oddly ominous, house. Inez's window was still open but from here we could hear nothing. In the dark window below hers a For Rent sign showed faintly. Below that was the basement apartment.

"If you have the murder method figured right," said Twit-Twit slowly, "she couldn't have done it very easily."

I nodded. "The shooting might be barely possible, of course. These old houses have pretty thick walls."

"But how would she get the body down two flights of stairs and into a car?"

"You have a practical mind," I said. "We'd be much better off if she lived in the basement. That opens directly on the street."

"There's still Eulalia."

"And Kim. And the Sinclairs. And the Kallikaks or whatever those Jackson Whites' names are."

Twit-Twit sighed and took my arm, as though to leave. But I could not help looking back and up at that open, silent window. What was she going through up there in that dark room? A torrent of grief? Or the shuddering terror of the guilty?

Then an indescribable thing happened. From that dark window came a man's loud voice—"Goes something like this"—then the bright tinkle of a piano rippling into the introduction of a song. It was "The Island of St. John," the song which Archie had said Rudolf Jersey wrote and Brillhart had stolen from him.

"That's pretty," Twit-Twit whispered.

I didn't answer. I couldn't have been wrong. The man's voice had been Brillhart's.

The chorus came to and end, and Brillhart said clearly, "It's rather a catchy thing, I think."

"Let's get out of here," I said.

# CHAPTER 2

*Special Delivery*

Next morning I put Brillhart out of my head, worked for four hours on the missiles story, and got it well started. At one o'clock I pushed the typewriter away, poured a sherry and, sipping it, thought about things. Then I went to the phone. A man answered at Eulalia Pope's number.

"This is Bill Deacon. Is Miss Pope in?"

"Oh, *Bill*." The voice was a cordial ooze. "This is Frank. How you been, boy?"

I wondered when we'd become engaged. "Fine, thanks."

"You're calling about the story, I hope?"

"That's right." Any lead-in would help. "I've been a little delayed by other matters, but now—"

"I know, I know. I saw your piece on resus—on resus—you know what I mean. Great stuff! I was fascinated. It was beautifully written."

"Thanks. I'd hoped to drop in on your sister sometime today for a little talk."

"She's recording this morning, Bill. You know how busy she is."

"Oh, sure. Well, a record should help her a lot. This is her first, isn't it?"

"Well...ah, a singing commercial is what it really is. For a cigarette company. One of the majors, of course. Look, I'm meeting her for lunch at the studio. Why don't you join us?"

"Why don't I pick you up at your place?"

"Great!"

\* \* \* \*

I asked the girl at the desk to tell Mr. Pope that Mr. Deacon was here and would like to come up and use his phone. Brother Frank's hearty welcome was audible from the switchboard.

The apartment was on the tenth floor of an eighteen story building, at the back and flanked by other apartments. It did not seem a likely place in which to fire a gun and expect it to go unheard.

"Sorry to be a nuisance," I told brother Frank. "I lost track of the time and if I don't call this guy by one-thirty—"

"Not at all, not at all! Use the phone in my bedroom. It's more private."

He led me past a bedroom door, through which I glimpsed boudoir lamps, a giant make-up table, and gauzy pink curtains, to another, more plainly furnished. He left me alone and I dialed the number of my own apartment. While I waited for me to answer I looked around.

This was a new building but it was not too substantially built, and certainly was not soundproof. While Frank had ostentatiously closed the bedroom door to give me privacy, when the front-door buzzer sounded I heard it plainly, and when Frank answered it I heard the few words that were exchanged. A bellboy had brought up a special-delivery letter for Eulalia.

I dropped the phone in its cradle and went back to the living room, which, aside from four large and dramatically framed photographs of the family's breadwinner, was furnished in the unimaginative style of apartment hotels.

"All set?"

"All set. I guess I missed him. Thanks for the use of the phone."

"Any time, Bill."

"Nice place you have here," I said. "But where's your music room? I'm just thinking of possible pictures, of course."

"If you want a picture of her at the piano—she plays beautifully, by the way—" he spoke tenderly—"that's easy. But we'll have to make it at the practice studio. She tried to practice here when we first moved in. God, the complaints! And Eulie doesn't even belt, you know. Her style is very intimate. But these new buildings are just cardboard—you know that yourself."

That took care of what I'd come to learn. But it occurred to me that if I eliminated many more living rooms I'd be fresh out of suspects.

In the cab I said, "The discovery of Brillhart's murder must have been an awful shock to your sister. I'm surprised she has recovered enough to work."

"Oh, Eulie's a trouper, and always has been, and this commercial is a big thing. Besides, she has a funny attitude toward the whole thing—sort of religious, you might say."

"Huh?"

"What I mean is, she's sort of let drop to some of us that she thinks Brill is still alive. It's like a religious faith. Matter of fact, I think learning the truth of his death was less of a shock to her than the days of uncertainty that preceded it. You see, his body was found just over a week ago. But he disappeared a full week before that—actually he was killed the night of the twenty-first, you see, at about eleven-fifteen. And what with his having disappeared once before, and knowing what had happened to him that time, Eulie just worried herself sick."

"Wait a minute. How do you know so exactly when Brillhart died?"

Chagrin swept the smooth face, eliminating its complacency. "I guess I shouldn'ta said that."

"But you did. How do you know?"

"I shouldn'ta said it. Especially to a reporter. Look, if you print it, you won't mention my name, eh? You could get me in a hell of a bind. And it'd be bad for Eulie."

"Then where did you get it?"

"From the cops. They know when he was killed, all right. I learned that when they questioned Eulie. They were checking alibis, see, and they were trying to find out who last saw Brill alive. Apparently it was Eulie. That's how it all came out."

"Tell me about it."

He looked uneasy. "Well, I will—as a friend. But for God's sake keep our names out of it. You can see why."

"Sure."

"Well, it was like this." He moved over closer to me, so the cab driver would not overhear.

"The night of the twenty-first, as I well remember, was the night of that big two-hour TV show for one of those diseases—you know? A benefit. Anyway, a lot of young talent was to be on it. Eulie and this Kim Winter and quite a few others."

"And were they?"

"You didn't see it?"

"I'm afraid not."

"Well—Eulie was great—she broke them up! She did 'Hey There.'"

"And Winter?"

"Winter was okay too. But anyway air time was nine and a little before eight Eulie and Brill had a fast hamburger together."

"He must have lived on them."

"Huh?"

The cab had reached our destination in the West Thirties, a building that looked as though it once might have been a mosque. We got out and I paid off the cab. "Finish this before we go in, will you?"

"Sure." We stood on the sidewalk, in the warm spring sun. "Well, that hamburger was important. Eulie goes on to the TV studio but Brillhart goes uptown. He says he'll try to see the show but he has to go up to Rockland County that night on business."

"*What?* What kind of business?"

"Brillhart didn't say. But it was monkey business, if you ask me. You never could believe what he said, although Eulie did, of course. He jived her plenty, poor kid. Anyway they left each other about eight-fifteen and that's the last time she sees him. Or anyone does."

"Not quite, apparently."

"Yeah, I see what you mean. Well, anyway, this cop, Cohen his name is, later gives us the rest. Brill's body is found out in a lonely field in Rockland County, as you know. And they estimate it was there a week."

"But things like that are always estimates, especially when the body is left outdoors. How could they pinpoint it?"

"Cause they've got more to go on. For the night of this TV show, which is just a week before Brill was found, somebody called the New York police and said there was this dead man lying out in a held, and gave them the approximate location. So the New York police relay this to the local cops in Rockland County. They go out and check, but either they don't try very hard or the directions aren't right, because nothing is found and everyone thinks it's some crank that called. Then a week later the body is found and they begin to piece it together."

"They get the time of the murder from that? Like hell they do if that's what Cohen said—"

"He said more. Listen, boy. The autopsy showed that Brill had been killed about three hours after he ate. They tell those things by the digestion or something. They examine their stomach—you know what I mean."

"I know what you mean."

"That puts it around eleven of the night he ate the hamburger. And there's something else about a surveying gang that found the body. They'd been working in that area some days before, I gather. I didn't quite get it but the whole thing adds up, according to Cohen."

"Anyway, it sounds like Eulalia has an alibi, if she was on television. And Kim Winter too."

"Oh, sure. Not that they need one." Brother Frank laughed. "Eulie's still nuts about Brill, and I think Kim went for him pretty strong, too."

"I suppose you're right."

"I know I'm right. In fact, the whole subject came up some nights ago at Inez's housewarming. She moved into a new place—a dump—up in the West Seventies, and asked us over for a drink. The gals got talking about what they were doing the night Brill was killed. The only one who didn't have an alibi was Inez. She was home sick, though I gather Kim talked to her on the phone that night."

"I see." I thought a moment, because something had occurred to me. "Were Eulie and Brillhart going to get married?"

"Hard to say," said brother Frank, and turned into the building.

In contrast to the building's exterior, the recording studio he led me to was a marvel of gleaming modernism. In the small control room where we dropped our coats an earphoned engineer fiddled with dials and switches at an enormous control panel and two big mahogany speaker enclosures stood in opposite corners like up-ended coffins. One wall was a broad glass window looking down on an auditorium ten feet below us where an orchestra was assembling among scattered microphones, the speakers reporting murmurs of their conversation.

Curled on a long bench in the control room was a slender little girl who looked about twelve. She was wearing toreador pants, white shirt and incongruously big, jeweled spectacles. She was frowning over the pad of paper on which she was writing and I had to look twice at that tinsel gold head to recognize Eulalia.

"Look who I brought, hon," said brother Frank.

She looked up, tapped the pencil between her teeth, and extended a hand. "Hi, Mr. Deacon."

"Sorry I'm late, Andy," brother Frank told a man standing nearby. "I just couldn't get here sooner."

"I didn't know you weren't here," the man said.

"You look like a little girl doing her lessons," I told Eulalia.

She laughed, pleased. "I'm writing my boyfriend."

Well, this didn't take long. *"Who's the lucky man?"*

She looked up, surprised. "I thought you knew. Brill Brillhart."

For a moment I was silent. I think I am hard to surprise. It can be done, though.

"You gotta move the mikes," the engineer said. "I can't filter it all out."

"Ah...and where do you write Brill?" I said.

"You think I'm crazy, don't you? All my friends do. But I'm not. Because, you see, I know better than they do, and you do. I *know* Brill is still somewhere—out there, somewhere, I don't know just where. But he'll come back to me someday, just as he did before. I know he will." She turned back to her pad. "Do you mind if I just finish this? I won't be a sec."

Through the speaker a piano sounded its A and the brass and the strings picked it up with blares and squeaks. You could hear the floor director. "All right, fellows, we'll run through it a couple times just for size and then try for a good clean take the first time out, right? How's the mix, Charlie?" He looked up at the control room.

"I haven't got the brass yet."

Eulalia bent over her letter and I felt sorry for her. She'd really been in love, all right. *Had* been? Still was.

"All right, Miss Pope," came over the speaker. She scrawled a hasty signature, threw down the pad, smiled happily at me, and started out.

"Just one thing," I said, and stopped her. "You didn't answer my question. How do you send letters to Brill?"

"Just like to Santa Claus when I was a little girl," she said. "I write them and seal them and then burn them. The smoke carries the message to him."

"And he gets them that way?"

"Of course he does," she said simply. "He must."

A minute later her blonde head appeared in the auditorium below and she wended her way through the musicians, scattered so irregularly for recording purposes, to a microphone standing beside a screen. On the other side of the screen a male quintet had assembled. The engineer near me made last-minute adjustments.

The director raised his fingers, the murmur from the loudspeakers in our small chamber became silence, and then trumpets chorded ear-splittingly. There was an intricate weaving of cymbal crashes and triple-tongued brass, a low harmony from the quintet, and then Eulalia sang, brightly swinging it, smiling invitingly:

"Oh, the Tipless Filter cigarette
Is the smoke for folk of action,
It's long, not strong, but nice as spice,
So it gives you satis—"

"Oh, balls," said Andy beside me.

He waved and yelled, "Cut it, cut it!" into an intercom. The music stopped. "Quintet, we can't hear you at all. Eulie, you were thin on the word *spice*. And for Christ's sake the rhythm section—"

They tried it again. And again.

And then again.

It seemed like a lot of trouble to take just for a singing commercial that no one would want to hear anyway except the sponsor. Finally the engineer took off his head set. "It's like I told you at breakfast, Andy," he said. "You gotta regroup 'em. It's a way-out arrangement and a nuts combo to begin with."

Andy nodded gloomily. "Then let's do it. We only got two hours."

Brother Frank beamed at everyone. "Eulie really came across, didn't she?" Andy just looked at him.

While he went down to superintend the shifting of orchestra and quintet Eulalia came back up into the control room. "You were great, kid," Frank told her, and added, to everyone else, "She was great. As always, of course." She smiled and picked up her pad and tore the several handwritten pages off it. I wondered if she would burn them now.

"Who were you writing?" asked Frank.

"Brill," she said.

Frank looked at me uncomfortably. "Sort of a whimsy, that's all," he told me.

"It's no whimsy," she said sharply. "Someday you will find out why."

"Sure, honey." Frank wanted to get her off a subject that could be an embarrassment in print.

She turned to me. "You and Frank should come to Inez's tonight, if you have no faith. We are going to have a session, all of us. We'll hear from Brill. Just as we did when he disappeared before."

"Sure, honey," Frank said again irritably. He reached into his pocket. "Here. I almost forgot. Here's a special came for you at the apartment just now."

As her long scarlet fingernail ripped the envelope, I said, "By the way, Miss Pope, when you last saw Brillhart, I understand he said he was going to Rockland County, on business."

"That's right. He said he had an appointment that night, a real big deal that he had going. He didn't ever say what it was but he hinted more than once that there was big dough involved. And, of course, it *had* to be way out in Rockland that night! Otherwise he never would have missed my telecast. He said so."

From the envelope she took out a small sheet of paper, and through the loud-speakers came a monosyllable from one of the musicians which I rather hoped she didn't hear.

She uttered a little cry. She looked up from the paper, her eyes wild with hope, and her mouth worked.

"It's Brill," she cried. "My God, it's from Brill!"

She began laughing hysterically and tears literally spurted down her cheeks.

"For Christ's sake, Eulie!" Frank said.

He took the paper from her. I looked over his shoulder. She sank down on the bench, laughing and crying and rocking back and forth.

What I read, in a bold florid handwriting, was:

My Dear:
   You think you know what has come between us and why I am not around so much. You don't. You haven't seen me because I am bored—*bored!* That is the plain truth.
   I am sure you will think there is someone else. There is, but there isn't. There are dozens—and there is no one. It isn't that I have someone else, at least at the moment. It is that I am tired of *you.* I won't mind if this leads you to do something rash.
   All good wishes, otherwise, from—

—Your Brill

I picked up the envelope she had dropped. The note was written in bright blue ink, with a broad-stubbed pen on plain white notepaper. The address on the envelope, also plain, had been typewritten. It was postmarked the day before, at Grand Central postal station.

Eulalia was looking up at us, smiling too brightly to be sensible.

"Do you know what that is?" she cried, and her voice began to rise as she spoke. "It's a letter from Brill—from *Brill!*" She screamed it and she screamed the rest, filling the small room with shrill hysteria. "He's alive—he's alive! He answered my last letter!"

"It's some practical joke," said Frank huskily. He looked frightened.

It occurred to me that it was not exactly a love letter.

Eulalia began to scream again and laugh at the same time; it was horrible and there seemed no way to stop it. The engineer yelled, "Rehearse somewhere else, will you, God damn it?"

But Eulalia continued rocking and laughing and uttering steady screams. Frank put an arm around her. "Now take it easy, hon. We got a tape to cut, remember?"

That had no effect. But when I asked, "Could it be a forgery?" that stopped the screams.

She looked up at me spitefully. "You think I don't know his handwriting? *His?* That was written by Brill. And to me. Because of what I wrote him."

"What was that?"

"A couple days ago I wrote him that I missed him so and wondered where he was and wished I knew. And I said, sometimes I thought of killing myself because I missed him so much."

"Now, hon!" That really scared Frank.

"This is his answer. He wants me to know he is all right, and will someday tell me where he is, and doesn't want me to—to kill myself." She looked ceilingward with bright, tear-washed eyes. "I won't, darling, I won't." The note slipped from her fingers.

"Jesus Christ," said the engineer.

I picked up the note. Frank was trying to dry her face, uttering soothing words. "Sure, hon, sure, but we gotta pull ourselves together, eh? We got work to do."

I slipped the note and envelope into my pocket. I said, "She's not going to feel like lunch. I'll ring you tomorrow morning."

"Sure she will, Bill," said Frank. "Hang around. Why, she's just—"

But I waved good-by from the door. I wanted that note for myself, even though I knew she'd soon discover it was gone and would know who took it.

# CHAPTER 3

## *The Doornail*

It was almost two and the Chalet Suisse' luncheon crowd had thinned out when I slid behind a table, and nodded to the unspoken question of Rene, the bartender. I could still hear Eulalia's screams ringing in that control room. Rene made a very dry Martini, thoroughly twisting the lemon peel over it, and after the first long sip I began to feel like thinking about things.

I took the note out and looked at it. I did not believe Eulalia's identification of the handwriting for an instant. It did not come from Brillhart, nor did it indicate in any way that he was alive somewhere. Brillhart was dead—as dead as Marley and the doornail. But who had forged it? Who had played so cruel a joke on a grieving little fluff-brain?

When I had finished my cocktail I looked up the phone number of the Manhattan East Homicide Squad and called Cohen. After the usual, "Who's calling him?" routine, I got him and told him what had happened, that I had the letter, and where he could get it if he was interested. He was. In fact, he thanked me so effusively for calling him that I concluded he did not know I'd been out of town. So I said, "Will you do me a favor?"

"Anything I can."

"How long do you think it will take for your handwriting man to figure out who wrote this?"

"It's a matter of comparison, obviously, and we don't have samples from many of the people involved. We've got samples of Brillhart's handwriting, and—well, a few others. I can't go any further than that."

"Can you go this far? I'm in a restaurant where I'm going to have a leisurely lunch. If you get any reply that you can share with me, would you ring me here—or at home this evening, if the answer comes later? I know I have no right to ask this. But I'm curious. And I didn't have to steal that letter for you."

"I'll see what I can do," he said.

It seemed I had hardly hung up before a man walked in from Fifty-second Street, looked around and came to my table.

"Mr. Deacon? Mr. Cohen sent me over for that little paper you mentioned."

"Here it is. Thanks."

"Thank you, Mr. Deacon. Cohen said to tell you he'd be in touch."

"Right." Watching him leave I wondered how many people appreciated the innate tact of the experienced New York cop.

\* \* \* \*

I had a good lunch, but 3:30 came and went and there was no call from Cohen. I had decided to leave and hope for word in the evening when a man came in, whom I could not see clearly against the bright light streaming in the front windows. Then I saw it was Cohen.

"Hi. Have some coffee."

"I will at that. Had no lunch."

"Busy day?"

He grinned. "You made it so, and thanks for that."

"Handwriting identified?"

"Yes. Our guy had no trouble at all. That's why I came over instead of calling you back. There are a few points I wanted to clear up personally. This is going to sound rude, Mr. Deacon, and I apologize in advance but—you saw this letter arrive, did you? It really came through the mail this morning?"

I thought.

"No. I didn't *see* it arrive. I saw it opened, and I don't think there was any sleight of hand." I told him the story. He listened, frowning.

"Now, let's share the wealth," I said. "I've told you. Why don't you tell me? Who wrote the letter?"

Cohen put his jaw in his hand, leaned forward, and spoke through the fingers laced over his mouth. "Our man, who's an expert—he's never been knocked down in court—had no trouble at all. And he swears he cannot be mistaken. The letter, which was postmarked yesterday, was written by Brillhart."

\* \* \* \*

I sipped coffee I did not taste and studied the tablecloth. I had expected any of four or five answers. Not this one.

"Do *you* think he's alive, Mr. Deacon? *Still?* " I couldn't tell whether he was baiting me or was serious.

"Not if the autopsy and fingerprints and all the rest mean anything. Don't they?"

"Sure they do. But I wondered what ideas you had. It's the second time around, you know."

"I know. But this is a different time around. The guy's dead and buried. Period. So barring resuscitation—But there's another explanation for that letter. I can think of several."

"Of course. So can I. And you're right about the fingerprints and autopsy. Brillhart's dead. No doubt of it. By every scientific test, he is dead. And yet..."

"And yet what?"

"He keeps cropping up."

"Not really."

"His car was found in Jersey this morning."

"What?"

"It's an old MG. It was in a used car lot that specializes in sports cars, and they have six or eight MG roadsters at the moment. Someone had simply driven the thing in there with the other roadsters and the management didn't notice it until this morning. They don't know how long it was there. Fairly unbusiness-like people, I take it."

"You're suggesting Brillhart drove it there?"

"Not exactly. There were two bullet holes in the door curtain on the driver's side."

"I see."

"Then there's the suit."

"Suit?"

"On the day Brillhart apparently was murdered his lawyer filed a rather cryptic damage suit against the estate of Rudolf Jersey. For a million dollars."

I thought about that for a while, too.

"It just came to our attention," Cohen said, "although it's a week old. Apparently he has a chance of collecting, too. Or did have. His lawyer is a shyster named Goall. Pretty well known as a shakedown specialist. Works on a percentage."

"That would figure."

"Sure. But Brillhart keeps alive, doesn't he? And he had lots of enemies. But only a limited number of them could actually have caused his death."

"And they all have alibis for the time of death," I said. "Except me. I don't know what I was doing the night of the twenty-third. Practically everyone else does though. Because of the television show."

"Oh? Who have alibis?"

"You know better than I. Kim and Eulalia for sure."

"Kim Winter probably. Eulalia certainly not."

"She was on the television show."

"You see it?"

"No. I wasn't watching television that night, if you're checking. I'll have to look up in my Boy Scout diary to find out what I was doing."

Cohen smiled faintly. "I didn't see the show either. But we've studied the kine at some length. Miss Winter came on early and sang 'I Concentrate on You.' That was about nine-twenty. Miss Pope was a stand-by and the singer she might have filled in for was there and also went on—about nine-thirty. Miss Pope never appeared in the show. There was a lot of confusion, as there always is at these unrehearsed marathons, so either girl could have put in an appearance, left early, not been missed, and even come back later, thus seemingly establishing that she was there all the time."

"Well—what do the two girls say they did?"

"Eulalia Pope says she stayed at the studio until almost eleven, hoping she might get some kind of chance to go on. She never did. Kim Winter says she hung around a little while after doing her song, went to the Copa for a bite, then home, had a bath and a massage by her maid, got a call from Inez Low, and went to bed. Miss Low confirms the phone call, incidentally."

"It's nice of you to be frank. What's Miss Low's own alibi, if any?"

"She doesn't have one. She says she had some sort of twenty-four-hour virus and felt so badly she could not get to the studio to help Miss Winter, whom I gather she had been coaching. So she stayed home, watched the show on television, and phoned afterward."

"Not exactly ironbound."

"No. Though when I talked to her she referred to the fact that the Winter girl flatted a B toward the end of the song, and also transposed some words in the lyric. The kine proves she did."

"From where I sit we're running out of suspects."

"Oh, no. There are others."

"The hillbillies who held him prisoner?"

"It's possible. His body was found in their bailiwick. Then there's your friend Sinclair."

"You don't have to worry about Archie."

"I do, though. I talked to him early in the game, but only briefly. Now I've other things to see him about and he's hard to find. His wife reports him out, and doesn't know where he is. If you hear from him—"

"Oh, sure."

"Brillhart had a lot of enemies," Cohen said thoughtfully. "But while many people hated him sort of generally, I don't know of any who could have killed him. The person I'd really like to see is that blonde who tried to get into his apartment some weeks ago."

"Have some more coffee."

"Thanks, no. I've got to run."

I had just started toward the office when it occurred to me that the sooner I warned Twit-Twit the better. There was no drugstore or other phone booth handy so I turned back rather abruptly for the restaurant, to phone there.

I didn't notice at first; I just brushed past another pedestrian, almost bumping him, dodged back into the Chalet Suisse, got to the phone, dialed, and heard no answer. That was that.

Once more I started for the office. I'd reached the lobby when I thought: she probably was out for lunch and could be back now. I wheeled around again and started back for the lobby telephones.

This time the pedestrian I had brushed past earlier was waiting for an elevator, at a distance. He looked at me, then looked ahead.

I dialed Twit-Twit's number and there was still no answer. But from the phone booth I could see the pedestrian, waiting for elevators and not taking them. He walked across the lobby and stared into a plate-glass window as shiny as a mirror. For him it *was* a mirror. He could see me in it.

Cohen had been nice. He had come over personally to see me at the restaurant, and he had even given me some news (but how much had he withheld?). In any case, he had really made sure that I was correctly fingered.

Now I was being tailed.

I hung up thoughtfully.

\* \* \* \*

I suppose being shadowed can become fairly routine, especially if you are a criminal trying to evade detection. I wasn't a criminal and I wasn't trying to evade anything. I just wanted to keep my friends out of trouble, especially Twit-Twit. And myself, if I could.

But being tailed is uncomfortable because it makes you suddenly realize that the simplest, most natural thing you might do, like ducking into a building to buy gum, or stooping to retie a shoelace, can look suspicious to the person watching you. And I'd already done enough, with my sudden turn-around. I did not want to do anything that might seem more suspicious, and I could not stay all afternoon in the phone booth. I walked out, not looking across where he was, and headed slowly, casually toward Fifth Avenue, making myself easy to follow.

I have never felt so self-conscious. A man wants to live in privacy, no matter how innocent he is. He does not like knowing that no matter if he even goes to the park and feeds bread to the pigeons, it will all be duly recorded that night in a report, badly typed on a typewriter with a light-gray ribbon: "At 3:34 subject proceeded by way of Fifth Avenue to Central Park..." Your natural impulse is to shake the tail, and yet you do not want to shake him at all, because that would be highly suspicious. Then you begin to worry about losing him, inadvertently, and you wonder how good he is (this guy was obviously awkward), and you hope he won't lose you and turn in a false report on you to excuse himself.

Finally you tell yourself that you should tear up a newspaper in small pieces and leave a paper trail for him, to make it easier for the damned fool, but what you ultimately do is head for home. At least that is what I did. All the way I swore at Cohen and hoped that the dumbbell behind me would not lose me.

\* \* \* \*

I got there about four. I tried to work but I couldn't. After a while, by approaching the front window from the side, I looked out. Down at the corner two men were standing; one was my friend. His relief had arrived.

I wanted to call Twit-Twit but I didn't dare. The phone might be tapped, too. What the hell had I got myself into?

Finally I lay down on the bed.

At five-thirty the phone began to ring.

\* \* \* \*

Quite a few years ago when I worked on a paper in the Midwest we had a reporter named Lansing. We had him briefly. I guess every paper in Chicago and Detroit, Milwaukee and Toledo had him, and always briefly. In case you don't know, the newspaper business is one with a fairly broad mind. You don't expect the other guy working with you to think or work or go to church or write the way you do. But one thing you do expect, and you should. You have a right to expect that he'll be honest with the people he's working with, and he'll always hew to the line of decent journalism, which means he will never betray a confidence, or turn in a friend, or pass the buck. Lansing did all these things, which is why he never stayed long on one paper. I once saw a committee of five good reporters walk into the managing editor's office and announce that if Lansing stayed on the payroll they were resigning. A couple of years ago he had turned up in New York and I'd occasionally seen his by-line.

When I picked up the phone now, a voice said, "Deac? This is Lindy Lansing. Remember me? How are you, kid? Gotta few questions for you."

I can't remember what I said but it doesn't matter. Lansing talked fast.

"You had lunch today at a restaurant on West Fifty-second, right?"

"Right."

"Good, good." He sounded happy. "And afterwards when you left you walked south and then doubled back. Why—did you figure you were being tailed?"

I had the good sense to keep my mouth shut.

"Whatsamatter—I'm not wrong, am I? You admit you were there and that's what happened?"

"I admit nothing."

He laughed. "You don't have to. You said you were at the restaurant. Everything else fits. Look, kid, play a little ball, and we can both do right well. I know what you're up to."

"Then why don't you tell me? All I want right now is to take a nap."

He laughed again, but now the laugh had a deliberate note. "The hell you want to take a nap. Not now, you don't. Listen, stupid. I was in a certain deputy inspector's office on Centre Street about twenty minutes ago. I happened to see something on his desk that I was not intended to see—a fresh report from the homicide bureau. There were names and addresses mentioned and I recognized yours. Now—do you want to tell me why you're a suspect in the Brillhart murder? Because if you will we can do business. I've got a good story right now and it's exclusive. But you can sweeten it up, even more. And I can help you in return."

I told him what he could do. I think it surprised him. But after I hung up I was worried. About a lot of people, including myself.

The phone rang again. A hoarse voice, not quite like a man's, said, "The golden hat. Without fail. In fifteen minutes. Got it? Emergency."

I said, "Got it. What gold hat?"

"There's only one, stupid. *Emergency!*"

"What the hell is this?"

The voice became agonized. "Be there, God damn it. Fifteen minutes. *Emergency.*"

The phone clicked off. But I had recognized that guttural. Twit-Twit was scared as hell.

So was I. What was I to do? She expected to meet me in fifteen minutes and if I did not get there something really disastrous might just possibly happen. But if I did go there I would lead the police to her. I sidled over to the window. A few doors away a man in a car seemed to be reading the paper. He glanced up. I sidled back.

I needed an idea. I went to the kitchen and poured a drink. I got an idea. I drank the drink. Either it or the idea made me feel hopeful. I got a manila envelope from my desk and filled it with yesterday's newspapers. Then I took an office label and wrote JONES MSS. on it in letters legible 100 feet away. I put on my coat and hat and practiced with the envelope before a mirror for a few minutes. Then I walked out and, on the sidewalk, looked elaborately up and down the street for a cab, although the sensible thing was to walk over to Sixth for one. Meanwhile I held the envelope under my arm in such a way that no one could miss that lettering. The man in the parked car did not.

Finally a cab came through Twelfth Street and I went off to La Cloche d'Or. There were only two customers in the place. One was finishing a meal at a table and the other, at the bar, was Twit-Twit, a dark-blue cloth coat with a cowl pulled around her, a brandy float in front of her. I took no chances on the joker at the table.

"Miss Jones, here's your manuscript," I said loudly and handed her the envelope. "I'm so glad you called, because the magazine is greatly interested in it."

"What crap is this?" said Twit-Twit. "Jesus Christ, Deac, am I screwed up! And am I scared."

# CHAPTER 4

*Pursuit*

Dig this.

She pushed a newspaper in front of me, but I looked around first. The man finishing his meal did not look like a cop; he was sipping coffee and reading a book. Outside a car had stopped on the other side of the avenue and the joker in it was poring over a paper. Everyone seemed to be reading. I did too.

It was the *Express* and the eight-column headline read:

TRAIL MYSTERY BLONDE IN BRILLHART MURDER

The story was by-lined, *By Lindy Lansing,* and next to it was a charcoal sketch of a flashy blonde with eyelashes an inch long and below it her description with the heading, *Have You Seen Her?*

The story read:

A major break in the mystery-shrouded Brill Brillhart murder occurred today when the *Daily Express* learned exclusively that the beautiful blonde who has long been sought as a key witness and possibly a suspect is still boldly prowling the East Side.

The *Express* immediately launched an intensive search for the woman in the area.

The information as to her whereabouts came from Albert Wojcik, superintendent of the apartment building where the noted songwriter lived and which the mystery woman apparently tried to burglarize some days before his death.

Wojcik spotted the woman about 8:30 this morning. She was walking on Madison Avenue near Fifty-sixth Street but he could not immediately follow her because he was on a northbound bus. By the time he got off she had disappeared.

"I am sure she realized she was spotted and so got out of sight," Wojcik told this reporter. "I am also sure of the identification."

The *Daily Express* has thrown all its resources into...

"That wasn't you," I said. "You never were up and out on the street at eight-thirty A.M. in your life."

"It was the only time I could get a hair appointment."

"Then get another appointment and have it dyed black. By the way, cloche means bell, not hat."

"Shut up. I figured the phone might be tapped. Because when I saw the paper after lunch, I went home and discovered there was a telephone man— at least he was apparently one—at work on some wires in the hall."

"It probably was a telephone man, doing something legitimate. These days phones are easier to tap than that."

"Great. Then mine's been tapped for days. Thanks for making my day."

She was genuinely frightened and that made me mad. There's no reason for anyone to frighten Twit-Twit, and I don't want her frightened. And now I had to scare her a little more.

"Keep your face turned from the front window. There's a cop outside, who's tailing me. I don't want him to see you."

"Are you kidding?"

"No."

She turned. I studied the charcoal sketch. The caption said it had been done by an *Express* artist from a detailed description supplied by Wojcik. It looked as much like Twit-Twit as I do, but still it was disturbing. It is not nice to know you are being hunted. I said, "Cheer up. It's a lousy likeness."

"It is not. The eyes are like me."

"You're crazy. But you shouldn't be around this neighborhood at all. It's just where they're looking."

"Deac. I'm in no mood to be picked on."

"Finish your drink and we'll get you to some place where it's safer."

"Home?"

"Not home. You can't tell what they might stumble on. You'll hide out for a day or two. I'll leave first to draw off the cops."

"Is that really what I should do?"

"The alternative is to surrender and tell the whole story. It's really a perfectly innocent story and no one can do anything to you for what you did. But it'll be messy at best, with a lot of publicity—especially with that God-damned Lansing encouraging that God-damned caretaker to keep the story alive. If we just keep you under cover the murder may be broken any minute. With the real killer in hand they'll forget all about you."

"And if it isn't broken?"

"We'll cross that spilled milk when we come to cry over it. Right now the thing to do is to get out of sight."

We were talking in low voices. The late diner had paid his check, taken his book, and gone out. As he did, there was a little confusion at the door because two men came in at the same time and they all got in each other's way in the small entrance hall. Then they came in, arguing a bit, and stood at the other end of the bar near the window.

"Don't think I'm buying a drink in every bar we hit," growled one of them. "My expense account isn't that big."

The other man chuckled. "I thought your newspaper made millions. You gotta admit checkin' the bars is a good idea. She was this type, I tell you, who would likely hang out in some of these places." They both looked around the place we were in and down at us.

They had just come in off the street and their eyes were not adjusted to the subdued lighting. They couldn't see us very well, and Twit-Twit's cowl was concealing. I could see them, though.

They were Lindy Lansing and the caretaker—and they were obviously combing the streets and bars for Twit-Twit. And in a minute their eyes would become adjusted. Outside the cop who was tailing me was still parked, seemingly occupied with the paper.

"You got two hundred from us for your story, and you get another three hundred if we find her," said Lansing. "So suppose you buy this one?"

I was between them and Twit-Twit. I leaned forward and turned so they would see less of her. "Do what I say. Never mind why. Walk out into the kitchen and go out the back door. Find your way to the street, get over to Second Avenue and take a cab to the Dolans'. *Do it*—now!" I pushed her.

Twit-Twit is not slow. She slid off the bar stool and headed for the swinging door to the kitchen in the rear. I didn't dare look around to see what Lansing and the caretaker were doing. But once I knew she was well away I would have a chance.

I never got it.

The waiter saw her pushing open the door to the kitchen, and of course misunderstood. "No, no, it is the door on the right, madame," he called courteously. Twit-Twit, startled, turned and looked around. And the light fell on her face.

"*That's her*!" squealed the caretaker and started running in my direction.

I yelled, "Keep going," and jumped off my bar stool.

The caretaker charged into me. I blocked him with my body. He looked startled and then squealed even higher, "And here's that Pollock!"

It would take Twit-Twit time to get out of the back and well away, especially with a cop just outside. I would like to say that in this juncture I thought fast and cleverly. I didn't, though. I simply acted.

It happens I boxed a little in college. I don't know what I was trying to prove at the time, though I know what I did prove: that I have a glass jaw. I've never tried to hit anyone since my junior year. Now I did. I forgot about leading with your left, and footwork, the glass jaw, and also the body weave which the boxing coach once told me was the only thing I did right. I swung on the caretaker and landed fairly well on the side of his cheek.

It stopped him, and he staggered back and floundered into Lansing just behind him. I grabbed him by the collar and tie, pushed sideways and he fell down, leaving me a clear shot at Lansing.

Maybe it was just the way I feel about Lansing or maybe it was because Twit-Twit is my girl, or so I like to think. Or maybe the body weave somehow worked. Anyway I hit him too, and this time I landed on the side of his jaw and he didn't stagger back. He went down and stayed there.

I ran through the kitchen, past a wide-eyed chef, out into a courtyard, saw a door in another building that looked promising, opened it, ran through a hall and found myself on Forty-ninth Street and well out of sight of the cop in the car. Twit-Twit was across the street heading for Second Avenue. But behind her was a well-filled parking lot. My whistle stopped her and I ran across and led her between rows of parked cars until we were out of sight of the street.

I wanted to think coolly. Instead my brain flashed with headlines—the next edition of the *Express,* when they learned they had sighted the mystery blonde again, only let her escape, the police tail I had so worried about losing, and had now lost in the most suspicious way, what they would all make of the desperate Mr. Pollock and how long it would take them to find out who he really was, for the management knows my name in that restaurant, even if Lansing didn't recognize me.

Above all, how was I to get Twit-Twit out of this?

The kid running the parking lot answered that for me.

He pulled a black Ford two-door up two rows over from us, leaving the motor running, while he went over on the other side of the lot to get someone else's car. I took Twit-Twit by the hand, pushed her into the back of the car, got in the front, and drove it out of the lot. I didn't even look back.

I drove north a few blocks on Third, then turned right and into one of the parking garages in that area. The guy who ran it asked, "How long, Mac?" and I said, "All night," took the ticket from him, rubbed my hands around the steering wheel and then the door handle to smear fingerprints and left. A cab took us to the One Hundred and Twenty-fifth Street Station and let us out. We went in for a few minutes, tried to become invisible by looking at the magazines, then walked out and took another cab to the Dolans'. That's only half a block from Twit-Twit's, but as long as she stayed indoors it could be the other side of the moon.

Betsy was there, thank God. It was nice to see how she recognized that Twit-Twit was frightened, and set about heartening her, even as I explained what was going on. As I did, I thought longingly of the Caribbean or Mexico. Or Brazil. Especially Brazil. You can't be extradited from Brazil. Maybe

Betsy read my mind. She said I needed a drink and didn't wait for me to get it at the dry sink under the gun collection. She poured it herself. It was a drink.

I thought a moment—it's odd how much you can think about when you have to—then went to the phone and dialed Archie's number. No one answered and I dialed it again; I could have misdialed, especially at that point. No one answered.

Then someone answered, a soft, calm woman's voice. "Yes?"

"Mary?"

"Yes. Archie?"

"Bill Deacon. Isn't Archie there?"

"No. He's—he's out."

"When can I reach him, Mary? Where, right now?"

"I don't know." Suddenly she didn't sound calm.

"When he comes home, tell him to call me at Tom Dolan's, will you?"

I probably wouldn't be there, but I was curious as to Archie's whereabouts.

"Deac?"

"Yes,"

"He wasn't with you today, at all?"

"No." I wondered how much I was jamming him up. Plenty, if he had said he was with me. "He's been gone all day?"

"Just about. I've been worried."

"I'm sure you'll hear from him soon." We rang off. Everyone seemed to be having problems.

I had my own, but they *were* my own. So I told Betsy to take care of Twit-Twit, to make sure she stayed indoors, and that I would call later.

Twit-Twit said she did not want to go out, and from the way she kissed me at the door she meant it.

* * * *

But going down in the elevator I wondered where the hell I went next. I knew where I wanted to go, all right. Home. But that was the last place I could go now, even if Lansing had not recognized me. If he had, what a lovely time he would have in print with "Mr. Pollock." Then there was that little matter of the briefly stolen car. I would mail the parking ticket to the police. But right now—

And there at the apartment entrance was the guy I most needed to help me. Dolan opened the door with his key, saw me, and said, "Hi."

"Hi. I want to buy you a drink."

"I want you to buy me a drink. But since we're close to my house let me buy one."

"No. You can't go upstairs. Betsy's entertaining."

"Not the Fuller Brush man again?"

"That's what she said. He looked like Cary Grant to me. Come along. There must be a corner bar."

"There are two corner bars."

We found one of them and I told him the story, and also what I wanted to do. I said, "I have ideas about the whole thing. But to make certain I've got to go out there. Tonight. Want to come?"

Tom spoke slowly. "As I get it, Twit-Twit's in a jam. But you are also in a jam. And pretty soon people are going to find out that the two of you are close friends and not who you claimed to be. Then you're in a hell of a jam."

"That's right. Have another drink?"

"Deal me in—on the expedition and the drink too. You have one too."

"Not now. I've got to rent us a car—a good one."

"We won't depend on rented cars. My head writer just bought himself a new Corvette and he's nuts about it. I'll borrow it."

"Okay. Call Betsy and tell her you won't be home for dinner. Meanwhile I'll get some sandwiches and coffee to take with us."

"And," said Tom, "a bottle of cognac, old boy."

Tom's writer garaged his Corvette on East Eighty-fifth Street. Black, it was still redolent of the exciting upholstery-and-metal smell of new cars and its motor was well-bred thunder. While the garageman gassed it up I went to the telephone and called the State Police barracks at Cold Springs. I said my name was Wilson—I had no idea what alarms might be out by now for Bill Deacon, and Mr. Pollock was getting a little shopworn. But I gave the right name of the magazine.

"We're doing a picture story on the Brillhart murder. We want a photographer to shoot some pictures of the exact spot where his body was found. Is there anyone who could point it out to me?"

"Tonight?"

"I know it's short notice. But we have to shoot early tomorrow to make a deadline."

"Well... Sergeant McGrady will be going over that way later on. He was in on it from the start. But he'll just check in here about nine and then go right out."

"I'll be there. And thanks a lot."

The Corvette panted gently behind me. "If you'll drive," said Tom, "I'll break out the food. I had no lunch."

He opened the paper sack, and black coffee and pastrami scent filled the small car. "Smells wonderful!"

It was good to be driving, going someplace and doing something about what had been bothering me. Tom apparently felt it too as we whirled through Central Park.

"'Deacon and Dolan on the Trail,'" he said, munching.

"Or, 'The Rover Boys in Darkest Rockland.'"

"How far is it to this Cold Springs, as the crow flies?"

"They don't know. They've never been able to get a crow to fly there."

"No jokes like the old jokes. Why are we going again?"

"Because before I make any definite moves I want to talk to all the suspects. And look over the physical layout of—of where they live and where it happened and one thing and another. Like I said, I may know who killed Brillhart. But I still don't know exactly how, and that's important."

"It sure is. You're a hell of an excuse for a detective."

At seven o'clock the spars and cables of George Washington Bridge made a pale glitter against the sunset's afterglow. Traffic was light and with that motor humming in front of me I lost no time. When we had paid the toll I ate a sandwich, and sipped coffee one-handed. Then I gunned her. The Corvette jumped like a bee-stung deer.

Driving, I thought quite a lot. I think best when I'm traveling, or moving forward—perhaps because movement makes one conscious of the relationships between time and space. At least I began to figure how important the relationships of time were in respect to the things I had recently learned, and for the first time began to see their simple pattern. So when we got into Goodrich, a town whose name I'd completely forgotten and yet now remembered, and found there was only one diner on the main street I got a couple of ideas. I pulled the car up.

"Tell me something," I said. "Isn't there something called an air check—a record of what is broadcast on radio?"

"Radio?" said Tom. "I'm a television man."

"Radio."

"Sure there is."

"What's on radio on Thursday nights that involves information? Like news programs. That might deal with show people like Brillhart. Not after eleven o'clock."

Tom frowned. "Anything. Why—Oh, Watkins. Ten-forty-five."

"I should have known without asking. Look. You know about these things. I want to know what Belle Watkins broadcast that Thursday night when Brillhart was killed. Isn't she on your network?"

"No."

"Are there any other gossip-column shows on radio on Thursday nights?"

"No."

"Thanks for being helpful."

"I'm being helpful. Belle is the only one. Don't think I don't know air times. We work against them."

"Okay. I have a goofy idea. I want to know what the great radio columnist had to say that night Brillhart was killed. She comes on at ten-forty-live—right?"

"Right."

"Okay. Can you make a call and find out or something?"

"Probably. I'll have to pay a secretary to transcribe it. If one's around."

"I'll pay the freight. Make the call, will you? I have to go in this diner."

"I'll open the brandy, then make the call."

\* \* \* \*

The diner was small, with not many customers. I sat at the deserted counter and ordered coffee. When it came, I said, "Did you have a woman come in here a month or more ago, kind of early in the morning, who turned out not to have any money? She'd have been with a guy who left first."

"Maybe." The white stubble on the counterman's chin had needed shaving for some time. "You a friend of hers?"

"Maybe. She asked me to pay what she owes you."

He thumbed through some slips at the cash register and came back with one. "Two coffees and a hot ham san'wich. I let her have the san'wich because she said she'd been walkin' all night. Fifteen miles or so."

The check totaled 65 cents, was signed, "IOU Joanna Gammer, Drewsville."

"That's the one. Here's the money. I'll take the check."

"Much obliged, friend."

\* \* \* \*

Sergeant McGrady had not arrived when we got to the Cold Springs barracks, so we parked outside the building and took a surreptitious pull at the bottle. "Nothing like drinking under police protection," said Tom. The brandy was a burst of warm French sunshine.

Heavy boots crunched the driveway gravel and I opened the door.

"Mr. Wilson? I'm McGrady. Want to follow me? I don't have much time." He looked at the Corvette. "I guess you won't have much trouble."

I noted our odometer reading and swung in behind the white police car. We followed it out of town for five point three miles. Then McGrady stopped, pulling well off the gravel road we'd been on for the last mile. Except for the cars' headlights and engine sounds there was only heavy, black stillness. McGrady turned on a big hand lamp.

"He was right over here," he said. "This way." He led us into the field that lay along the road and down a slight slope. Perhaps fifty feet from the road there was a little rise and at the top of it he paused and flashed the big light to a spot about twenty feet beyond. Half a dozen white stakes made a pattern in the short weeds.

"They mark the position of the body," said McGrady matter-of-factly. But it was odd studying the pattern of stakes and knowing that big, blustering Brillhart had lain there, a dew-wet corpse. "You notice this little rise? That's why he wasn't found for a week. It barely hid him from the road."

"Is this spot far away from everything?"

"Oh, no. In the daytime this road gets a fair amount of traffic. We're only about five miles from town. Besides there were surveyors working here even on the day of the night he was dumped. They're mapping a new throughway exit, and when they came back a week later they were the ones who found him. I'd say it was more luck than anything else that he wasn't found before then. Does this do it for you?"

"It sure does, sergeant, and thanks for your trouble." We started back toward the car. "By the way, did you ever hear of a family around here named Gammer?"

He looked at me. "Sure. There's several Gammers in this area."

"Near this spot?"

"Not real near. Nearest one I recollect is over in the Drewsville neighborhood. That's a four-corners town and that Gammer family is somewhere up in the hills. Why?"

We'd reached the car. "Is one of them named Joanna?"

"That I wouldn't know."

"Can you tell me how to find their place?"

McGrady had switched off his big light but in the dim illumination of the dashboard I saw his face become professionally attentive.

"You weren't thinking of trying to find it tonight?"

"Oh, of course not."

"Because if you were, I can tell you, Mr. Wilson, that I myself wouldn't want to attempt it, even if I had another man with me. I don't know whether you know much about the hill folks around there—"

"I know a little."

"Then you know that they are hillbillies and would figure anyone prowling around their place at night was an enemy who meant to do them harm. They'd shoot first. They're more than tough. They're crazy. Stay away, especially at night."

"I get you. However, if I want to find these Gammers sometime later on, in connection with a story we've been thinking of, how'd I get there?"

"You'd drive into Drewsville and keep north on the main street—" He got out his notebook and sketched a map. It involved several turns on increasingly narrow and remote roads after Drewsville. "Then"—he handed me the map—"when you get that far, inquire of someone. That's the best I can do for you. The people you want wouldn't live on a road or anything like that. They're up in the hills."

"Thanks a hell of a lot, sergeant."

"Perfectly all right. But stay away from there at night."

# CHAPTER 5

*The Light In The Lane*

It was well after 10 p.m. when we reached Drewsville. In calling it a four-corners McGrady had exaggerated. It was a handful of houses strung along a two-lane highway. There was one filling station and it was closed.

I drove slowly, following McGrady's directions exactly. That wasn't hard. There weren't many roads to confuse me.

"Why are we doing this again?" Tom said.

"Lots of reasons."

"Most of them named Twickenham."

"Maybe."

"Then sail on, sail on, oh, ship of state. As long as the brandy holds out."

"Is it holding?"

"Take a reading."

He handed me the bottle and I took a reading. It was holding out.

The two-lane highway became a gravel road. There were a few houses. A turn took us on another gravel road, but narrower, where the houses were infrequent. Then we turned left onto a dirt road, very narrow, with no houses at all. The odometer said we were eight miles from Drewsville. It seemed like a thousand.

When we'd been flicked by branches for a while I said, "What do you think?"

"Whatever you say. If you want to, go on. What the hell—I can lick my weight in hillbillies!" He thought a moment. "Of course, I don't weigh much."

We went on.

After another ten minutes of blackness and uncertain ruts, I said, "It must be around here that McGrady said to stop and ask directions."

"Yes. He neglected to tell us who to ask, though."

We went on. The dirt road rose steadily and twistingly, taking us up into hills, forcing me to down-clutch repeatedly. Then we rounded a suicidal turn and there, incredibly, was a light—a lamp in the window of a small house. I pulled off the road as best I could and we both went up to knock at the door.

"Thank God they're awake."

"Watching television," said Tom. "Some of my far-flung fans."

"You shouldn't fling them so far."

The woman who suddenly opened the door held a baby with one arm. Her right hand was behind the door, and somehow I knew that it held a gun. "Whad you want?"

"I'm trying to find the Gammer family," I said. "I know they live around here but—"

"I ain't never heard of 'um."

"There's a lady named Joanna Gammer."

"I never heard of her. What for you want to find any Gammers?"

"Is your name Gammer?"

"No."

The contempt in her face told me this was the truth. I took a chance. "I want to find them because they think they're in some kind of trouble. I know they are not. It's about one of their women."

Her eyes were suspicious. The baby put wet fingers into its tiny mouth, choked on them, and coughed. The woman said, "Wait a minute," and closed the door.

I said, "We're going to be late for bridge at the Gammers'."

"You'd be surprised how well I could bear that."

The door opened again. The woman said, "Come on in." The interior was lighted by two oil lamps, one in the window and one suspended over a dining-room table in the middle of the small floor. The room was hot with the reek of oil and cooking. Two youngsters of eleven or twelve sat at the table holding hands of rummy and two more hands had been turned face down on the table; we had interrupted a family game. A smaller youngster sat up in a frowzy cot in a corner of the room, rubbing sleepy eyes, as we came in.

"Want some coffee?"

"No, thanks. If you could just give us an idea where the Gammer place is—"

"Thought I'd make some coffee for myself while we played cards. Sure you wouldn't like some?"

"Thanks, really. Is the Gammer place—"

The woman's stare was long and level. "You've missed it," she said. "You went past it. Back about two mile. Then up in the hills."

"How far up?"

"Mile, maybe."

Tom said, "Is there a trail or anything like that?"

The woman laughed.

"Sounds hard to find," Tom said, "especially at night."

"I wouldn't want to try," she said, "and I know where it is."

We looked at each other. "That's that," I said. "Well, thanks, madam. Sorry we disturbed your card game."

She said nothing. Neither did the kids. The gaze of all of them was heavy on us as we closed the door. The fresh air smelled good.

"Well, at least we have an idea where to find it," I said. "In daylight, that is."

I pulled the car into a lane a little beyond the house to turn around. As I did I saw, briefly, a speck of light far down the lane. It disappeared, then reappeared, jiggling slightly like a nervous lightning bug. Someone was walking down the lane carrying a lantern.

"Holy Michael," I said. "How dumb can we get?"

"What's the matter?"

"Didn't it strike you as odd that she suddenly got so hospitable and asked us in for coffee?"

"These people are nuts."

"Like hell. How many people were playing rummy at that table?"

"Three—no, four. There were two hands face down."

"Sure. One was the woman's. But who was playing the fourth hand? Not that kid in the cot. She'd just waked up. No—I'll bet you a million I'm right."

As I spoke I took a careful look at the narrow lane to memorize it as best I could, then switched off the headlights and started driving slowly down it after the lantern. "Where the hell are you going? This isn't the way back."

"Someone's going down this lane with a lantern. That could explain the delay at the door after we told her what we wanted. She sent someone—probably the oldest kid or whoever was playing the fourth hand—out the back to warn the Gammers while she first tried to delay us and then lied to us. The Gammers are near here."

"Gee. I'm glad!"

The lane was rutted but the tires wouldn't always stay in the ruts. A few stars became visible in the blackness but they didn't help. Then I caught sight of the lantern again, and it gave me a point of reference.

I concluded, "That guy or kid up ahead can guide us to where we want to go."

"We do? Okay. But why not stash the car?"

"Not until necessary. We may need it."

Branches and dried weeds raked the sides. The lantern disappeared again, then it blinked back into view, presumably as the walker emerged from a hollow. It was closer now and I stopped a moment so there'd be no chance of our engine hum reaching him.

The lantern made a sharp right turn and began to climb irregularly. I inched the Corvette forward and hoped there was road in front of it. The lantern bobbed and dipped steadily upward on our right.

"Either the lane turns in that direction or he's left it," I said.

"I think he's climbing a hill."

"That figures."

When I reached the point where the lantern carrier had apparently turned, I risked flashing the headlights on for just a second. The lane stretched on ahead.

"Looks like your deductions were right," said Tom. "He's taking to the hills, and we know why. Do we follow him?"

"First I'll turn the car around so we can make a fast getaway the way we came. Get out and guide me."

We gave the lantern time to get well out of earshot. Then it took a dozen backups and forwards to turn around in that narrow space, especially since I didn't dare race the motor. When we finally started up the slope the lantern had disappeared. As we emerged from the trees lining the lane, the sky seemed lighter out in the open, and we were able to walk fast up the boulder-strewn hillside. After a few minutes we sighted it again.

Now it was coming toward us.

There was no cover except the darkness, and suddenly that was not dark enough. There was something frightening and inexorable about that oncoming little circle of light, with no real hiding place from it.

I ran to the left and Tom followed me. "This way!" We flung ourselves down behind small boulders and hoped for the best. If the lantern maintained its course it would pass about fifty feet away. Peering out from behind the rock I held my breath.

It drew abreast of us and we could see who carried it—a pale, scared-looking, skinny boy of about fifteen. He passed on, puffing a little.

I'd raised my head to watch his course; suddenly I dug my nose into the ground. And hoped to heaven Tom had seen it too.

A tall, striding man had silently loomed up scarcely fifteen feet from us, paralleling the boy's course and carrying a rifle cradled in his arms. In the faint starshine I glimpsed a lean wolfish face, the head set forward hungrily. I've never been so scared. And I'm not ashamed of it.

Over beyond another quiet-treading figure, also with a rifle, moved like a flitting ghost. *How many of them were there?*

The nearer one did not see us. God knows why. But he spoke. "They're two men, remember," he muttered, "so they could be moving fast. Last time the woman had trouble getting up the hill. But men could be anywhere by now."

He meant us and they were looking for us.

What had happened rushed in on my intelligence, such as it is, like a swirl of cold surf. During the few minutes when we had lost the lantern the boy had reached the Gammer cabin and told them someone was looking for them. Now they were coming back with him, and with guns, to see who it was. Maybe they suspected he could be followed; hence the eighteenth-century outrider technique of following on his flanks at a distance. Or maybe the boy had heard our engine after all and told them. In any case they were between us and the car. And they had guns.

"Did you see them?" Tom whispered hoarsely.

"I wish I were in Condon's."

We waited awhile; apparently there weren't any more; then we started following them. This was easier because now the lantern was in plain sight. But I was scared I'd step on something like a dry branch and draw their attention. In New York even a professional gunman has a few inhibitions about shooting. Out here I couldn't think of a single inhibition that could bother anyone. I wasn't breathing well.

I didn't say anything to Tom. He didn't seem to want to say anything either.

It didn't go on forever. That's how it felt, though.

After a bit, they bore left, taking a short cut toward the house we had left. Finally they reached the lane, well away from the car, and began walking back toward the kid's house. We branched off the other way toward the car.

As we neared the lane, their lantern stopped. It looked, through the trees, as though they were holding a council of war in the lane. At least, they were not moving. And they were between us and the way back to the main highway.

"I had to be so damned bright and turn the car around."

"Forget it," Tom whispered. "Now we just turn it around again and go down the lane the other way. There must be another main road."

We had reached the fringe of trees and undergrowth lining the lane. We moved through it as silently as we could. Then we saw them clearly. About a hundred yards away—no more—the lantern stood in the middle of the road and they were standing around it. You could hear a faint murmur of argument.

"They'll sure as hell hear the motor."

"So we'll do it fast," said Tom. "Because they may start back this way any minute."

"How right you are."

I looked down the lane again to the little knot of lantern-lighted people. Someone's hands were moving argumentatively. Someone else's arms still held a rifle. "They suspect something but they don't know what it is," I said.

"And they have guns," said Tom. "Let's go. You drive."

We found the Corvette. A little breathlessly, I said, "You guide me. I'm going to turn fast. The instant I hit the starter they'll hear it. So, for Christ's sake, don't let me back into a ditch. Or run you down."

Cheerfully, Tom used two words to tell me what I could do.

I got in and took my time finding the various knobs and switches in the dark. And dark it was. I whispered, "Ready?'

"Ready."

I said, "Hang on to your hat," and twisted the starting key. The Corvette came to life with a little roar. I turned on the lights and backed fast.

"Stop!" Tom yelled. I stopped. I went forward. I stopped again and backed. From down the road I heard a yell. I twisted the wheel and threw it into first. I kept the motor racing and switched my foot between brake and clutch while my hand whipped the stick transmission insanely. I heard feet running toward us.

Then she was turned around, Tom jumped in and I gunned her. The lights showed a narrow lane ahead of us. I heard a shot from behind but nothing seemed to touch us. I kept my foot on the accelerator.

For two hundred yards.

The light illuminated a stone wall. I hit the brakes. There was no way to turn. The lane was a dead end. And it was still lined with the same small trees and underbrush.

I could imagine the lean, long-legged men coming after us, having re-loaded, knowing the terrain, running quietly.

Then I didn't have to imagine. I heard the soft footsteps.

"We turn around again," I said, panicked. "But faster. We're trapped. So, for Christ's sake—"

Tom was already out of the car. "Don't spill the brandy" was the last thing he said.

I began twisting the wheel. "Farther!...farther!" Tom yelled. "Whoa!"

Maybe the lane was wider here. Maybe I was more desperate. Or luckier. I did it fast.

During the last couple backs and forths our lights picked up the three of them, the boy behind the other two lugging the lantern, the men looking big and tough, the guns raised. When I flung the door open for Tom to pile in they may have been fifty yards away.

I hit the accelerator and the little car did a standing broad jump. "Keep down," I yelled, and the Corvette began to bounce.

I kept the lights on; there was no hope of concealment now, and I held the accelerator to the floor. They leaped for the sides of the lane. We did fifty-five in second.

I thought of strategy.

Jumping for safety, the kid had dropped his lantern in the middle of the lane. I knew where the two with the guns would be and what they'd be planning. I hit the brakes and switched out the lights. The lantern gave me a target. I braked down to half our speed, pointed the Corvette at the lantern and once more floored the accelerator.

I yelled, "Duck." As we got to the lantern I bent down almost to the transmission, driving blind, feeling the car buck wildly, hearing a tinkle of glass as we rode over the lantern.

Almost simultaneously, two guns barked, one hoarsely, one sharply.

Maybe we were going too fast for them, maybe they just fired late. I think, if I may take a bow, that my strategy threw them off somewhat. In any case we were a little past them when they fired and we were really moving. Something zinged against a window and I heard a strange sound like a burst of spray, and pellets rattled on the car. I felt a sting in my cheek.

Then I was up again. I flashed the lights back on, twisted desperately away from a tree on the left and kept the car bouncing down those ruts, thanking our stars it was so roadworthy.

"McGrady, where have you been?" said Tom. I heard a cork twist out of a brandy bottle.

We were doing sixty when I slowed for the road that we had turned off so shortly before. It seemed like a hundred years.

The car window beside me was an opaque glaze of broken glass.

I turned her on to the road and gunned her again, even though they were a long way back. I looked at Tom. "Okay?"

"Sure. But you'd better pull that piece of glass out of your cheek. Or slow down and I'll do it."

He did. It was a shard from the safety glass. "I could sterilize it with a little cognac," Tom said.

"Cognac is more effective taken internally."

He extended the bottle. "You're right."

"Lousy shots, weren't they?"

* * * *

We were halfway back into New York, and the cognac was gone, when Tom said, "Tell me, my dear Holmes, what are your theories of the case at this time? I gather you have some."

"As a matter of fact, I do. And as a matter of fact, our little exploration has helped to refine them and eliminate some suspects."

"I'm glad to hear that. Because up to now I was not sure what we had accomplished."

"I'll tell you what we've accomplished. We exonerated the Gammers."

"The *Gammers?* He jumped indignantly. "If you are going to exonerate those bloodthirsty bastards!"

"I'm not. They exonerated themselves. By their behavior tonight. Think a minute and see if you don't agree. If they had somehow kidnapped or lured Brillhart out there and killed him, their reactions when they learned someone was inquiring about them would be to run and hide out in the hills. Instead, they came down and met trouble head on. Why? Because they felt they had been wronged in the whole thing and their response was vengeful. They came looking for the people who, they'd been told, had talked of one of their women being in trouble. That's not the reaction of a guilty person."

"You may be right," said Tom. "Narrows the suspects, though."

"Sure. But also remember what that Dan'l Boone muttered about a woman getting up the hill."

* * * *

It was 12:30 when we drove the Corvette back into the garage. I wheeled fast past the night attendant so he wouldn't see the rifle hole in the top or the shotgun damage to the window.

We took a cab to the studio and Tom got the transcript. I skimmed through it under a street light. Halfway through the usual mish-mash of misinformation by the noted Hollywood columnist I found this: "...and her husband, Gary Cooper, are off to Paris again.... It looks to friends like the Jack Welch-Linda Laughton marriage is on the rocks...and even more on the rocks is Brill Brillhart's... Eulalia Pope says she and the song writer will croon Wedding Bells as soon as his lawyer makes with the legal jazz that will end his marriage to Inez Low..."

And that was that.

"Found what you wanted?"

"Yes. And kiss the girl who stayed late to type it, will you?"

"Kiss her yourself. It was Betsy. I couldn't find anyone free to do it at the studio, so she went over. Come on up to the house."

"I will, to thank her—but just for a moment. I still have things to do."

"Busy little man."

But when we got to the Dolan apartment not only Twit-Twit but Archie and Mary Sinclair were there.

And Betsy Dolan had a very odd expression in her wide blue eyes.

# CHAPTER 6

*The Final Appearance*

She put a warning finger to her lips.

"Hi, fellows," said Twit-Twit loudly. Twit-Twit does not speak loudly.

"What do you say, boy?" said Archie, who never calls me "boy."

Betsy Dolan pointed frantically to the closed bedroom door, through which came a mumble of conversation.

"What the hell goes on?" said Tom.

"Shut up, idiot," she whispered fiercely.

"What did you do to your face?" Twit-Twit asked, and sounded concerned.

The mumble in the bedroom stopped.

"We got slightly shot at," said Tom cheerfully. "But we proved something. Or so says the Deacon here. We drove up to Rockland—"

"Shut up," I said, and began to whisper too. "What *is* it? Aren't we among friends? Stop making motions, Betsy. They haven't nailed Twit-Twit, have they?"

"*Nailed* her," she repeated, leaned against the wall, dislodging two old playbills, and closed her eyes.

The bedroom door opened.

Lieutenant Hyman Cohen stood in it. His dark-blue suit had been pressed by an artist.

"Good evening, Mr. Deacon," he said. I introduced him and Tom, emphasizing the "Lieutenant."

"Lieutenant Cohen just got here," Betsy threw in hastily. It was valuable information. Did he know who Twit-Twit was? Presumably not. So I should get her out as fast as possible.

"Get your things on," I signaled her. "I'm taking you home, but now. I've got to be up early."

Cohen smiled a sad, understanding smile. "Sorry," he said. "I don't blame you for trying." Everyone grew very quiet.

He said, "We've had a man on Mr. Sinclair from time to time. He was on Mr. Sinclair tonight."

"So what? What right had you to barge in here? You haven't a thing against this girl."

"He didn't barge," said Betsy, obviously wishing he had.

"I got restless, darling," said Twit-Twit. It was the first time she'd ever called me that before anyone else. "So when Archie and Mary dropped by—he had to fly up to Boston, suddenly this morning—Archie took me for a walk. We thought at night, in the dark..."

As though I'd been there I saw the cop, who'd been tailing Archie, outside.

"Our man recognized Miss Twickenham," said Cohen. "He called in, and I came up. Mrs. Dolan was nice enough to let me come in."

Betsy raised a stricken face. "What else could I have done?"

"Nothing, once they knew where Twit-Twit was."

"You ought to be glad," Cohen said a little reproachfully, "we located Miss Twickenham before the newspapers. At least, we won't question her in public."

"Question her?"

"That's why I was on the phone just now. I'd like her, and you, Mr. Deacon, and also Mr. and Mrs. Sinclair, to come over to the Homicide Bureau, where a department stenographer is meeting us. I would like statements from all of you."

Not by a decibel had the soft voice changed. Yet suddenly he was ten feet high and threatening. He was The Law. You couldn't fight him.

"Why are you leaving out the Dolans?" said Tom. "We're as criminal as anyone. In fact, criminaler."

No one laughed. Twit-Twit's face was white and her small chin was set so it wouldn't tremble.

"Wait a minute."

I didn't know what I was going to say next. I didn't know how much I dared say.

Someone knocked at the door and Betsy went to it. "Car's in front, sir," a voice said behind me.

"Down in a minute, Cliff," said Cohen.

"How long have you known?"

"I reached my conclusions tonight."

Cohen spoke slowly. "I'll go along with you. I have to, if you have information. But I am not releasing Miss Twickenham. She'll ride in my car. With Mr. and Mrs. Sinclair."

"The Dolans will ride in Mr. Deacon's car," said Tom loftily. "And they will serve a drink before take-off." He headed for the kitchen.

As I helped Twit-Twit into her coat, she said, "This will be my first ride in a police car." She smiled but her voice trembled.

"You'll love it. They get interesting radio programs." I put my arms around her for a second. "I won't be far away."

She held my arms around her. "Do you really know who killed Brillhart?"

I didn't answer. Cohen I would lie to. Not her.

\* \* \* \*

The unmarked police car followed Tom, Betsy, and me down the street from the corner to Inez's house and double-parked in front of it. Dull light came from the half-open window of Inez's second-floor apartment. "That's the place," I told Cohen. "Let's see what goes on." The rest of them followed us in.

Again we had no trouble getting upstairs. Silence came from the other side of Inez's door. Then we heard the scrape of a chair.

"What are we looking for?" Cohen whispered.

I gestured for silence, and we listened again, for several minutes. That's a long time when there is a great deal at stake.

The silence was dramatically broken. From the other side of the door Kim Winter's voice drawled, "Oh, really, Inez. *Really!* Nothing's happening. It was silly from the start."

"You think so."

"It wasn't silly from the start." A young, tender voice, Eulalia's. "And it isn't. We'll hear. I know we will."

"She is right," said Inez. "He is near—as near as this little table. In fact, I could show you how near he might be." The scrape of a chair again, then silence.

Once again, as I had heard the night before, there was a mutter of male conversation. But now a piano rippled some introductory notes, then a man's laughing voice said, very clearly, "Well, if you insist, angel."

Kim Winter screamed.

A couple of chords sounded and then he began to sing, low yet clearly. The song was "The Island of St. John," which Archie had said Rudolf Jersey wrote and Brillhart had stolen. The man who spoke and had called Inez "angel" and who was now singing the song was Brillhart.

I couldn't be wrong. I knew that voice.

"What's going on in there?" Cohen whispered fiercely. I felt my flesh crawl. I told myself it was fatigue. Fear glared through Archie's telescopic lenses.

"That's Brillhart singing," he gasped. "I can't be wrong."

"It's Brillhart's voice all right," I said.

Cohen looked at both of us, irritated. "Once and for all, Brillhart is dead. Don't you understand that?"

"Sure," I said. "But he doesn't stay that way, does he?"

I knocked loudly on the door.

# CHAPTER 7

## *The Alibi*

Inez opened the door. She was wearing a flowered housecoat. She said, "My goodness," in a puzzled way. Then she said, "What's going on?"

A man stood behind her. It was brother Frank. Apparently he had just come for Eulalia, since he was wearing a coat and was holding hers for her. The party was breaking up. The Ouija board lay on a card table, pushed aside. There was no piano.

The people with me walked in too. The people in the small room looked bewilderment at us. All together, we filled the room. Presently some of them had to sit on the floor.

I said, "I hope you'll pardon the late visit. There's no statute of limitations on murder and so no limitation on the time when you arrest murderers."

I do not claim it was the world's best walk-on line, but it had the effect I wanted. Brother Frank said, *"What?"* Eulalia looked dumb and Kim puzzled. Inez was pale and Archie obviously uncertain.

I said, "It's nice everyone is here because everyone has a part in this."

"In what?" That was Eulalia.

"The arrest of Brillhart's murderer."

"He's not dead—you know that!" Her eyes glittered with tears and venom. "And where's my letter?"

Inez said, "Maybe I'd better make coffee."

I said, "This won't take a minute."

I looked around. This was the end—the end of Brillhart. "I know I should make this dramatic," I said, "but I can't. Maybe it's because once you see the events in their natural order it's too obvious to be dramatic. Anyway, I'll be brief."

No one said anything but Inez's eyes glittered.

"Brillhart needed money," I said. "So did Inez. I suppose they always did. There was no romance between them anymore—in fact, it was mainly hatred. But they had something in common. They were married, he owed her money, he had a way of getting money out of Jersey's estate, and she had a kind of blackmail threat over him. If she chose she could ruin his suit for damages by telling the world why Rudolf Jersey had tried to kill him. If he chose—and collected—he could pay her what he owed her. When an early effort to get money out of Archie here failed, Brillhart fell in with a shyster and filed a damage suit against Jersey's rich estate, based of course on Jersey's attempt to kill him. That's when the real action started.

"That's what I mean by chronology. For the suit did not come to light right away. But take it as the starting point and everything else follows, especially if you don't assume that certain similarities both in the Jersey murder attempt and in the actual killing of Brillhart were consciously arranged. You see, Brillhart was not killed in New York City at all but in Rockland County. As I will explain.

"Considering that Brillhart needed Inez's cooperation in his suit and she needed the money he owed her, it is hardly surprising that they might get together. She herself told me one day at my office that they were currently friendly and she told Lieutenant Cohen they were engaged in a mutual enterprise. She said it was a voice-coaching school, a fairly obvious lie to anyone aware of their real feelings toward each other. But they needed each other, and they also needed the testimony of the Gammers about the wounds Jersey inflicted on Brillhart.

"When Eulalia told me that he had talked of having a big 'business' appointment in Rockland County, I got an inkling. When Lieutenant Cohen here revealed the suit, things I'd learned out of context began to form a pattern. And the number of small, confirmatory facts was as astonishing. It was a woman who called the police on the night of that lonely murder and told them of it. It could have been one of a number of women, of course. But who, having killed him, would want his body discovered? Inez. She wouldn't want that million-dollar suit to die for lack of a corpse, since she stood to inherit, and she didn't want to wait seven years to inherit, either. So who came to my office and tried to interest me in finding Brillhart? Inez. Who could have a letter, actually written by Brillhart and expressing contempt for her, and also have wanted to send it out of sheer spitefulness to the girl he had most recently loved? Inez. Who, as the victim of nerves and remorse, and fear of discovery, might weep hysterically in the night? Who had the strongest, most practical motive for wanting Brillhart dead and wanting his death discovered? The answer is always the same. Inez."

\* \* \* \*

Her normally dark face was the color of pale cream and its harsh lines were venomous.

"This is an open accusation," I said. "You killed your husband, Inez. Out of long-standing hatred, sparked by a sudden turn of events." Everyone heard her suck in her breath. "Personally I wouldn't care much one way or the other, but too many other people are becoming involved."

"Killed him?" Eulalia was on her feet, screaming. "You—Inez—you *killed* him?" At long last Brillhart's death had struck home. "And *you* sent me that letter? You are—"

Brother Frank pulled her back down on the couch almost brutally. "Easy, hon. We gotta keep our heads now. It's all over now." She put sudden hands to her face and wept in them loudly.

I wasn't liking any of it. "I'm not through yet," I said.

"I'll say you're not," said Kim Winter. She crushed out her cigarette. "If you are accusing Inez of killing Brill the night of the telecast you're nuts. And I can prove it."

Inez sighed. "Thanks."

"Go ahead. Prove it."

"After Brill's disappearance Inez coached me," Kim said. "The night of the telecast she had the flu and felt awful, so she watched the show at home. But she called me to give me a pat on the back later. Inez was at home watching the TV show that night. I know."

"Tell us how you know."

"After I went on I hung around the studio with friends awhile, then we dropped over to the Copa for supper, and then I went home. She called a little after midnight and she told me I'd fluffed a lyric, which I knew I had, and she said I'd hit the high part of the release in 'Concentrate on You' very well."

"Had you?"

"I fluffed, all right."

"I'm sorry," I said. "You were fooled, and some other people were by the fact that Inez has a tape recorder, naturally enough for someone in music coaching. She even has some tapes of Brillhart playing and singing, as Miss Twickenham and I heard before and we all heard again tonight. You were her student, Kim, and even though she pretended illness to devote the evening to something far more important to her, she would naturally want to hear how you did. She had only to set her tape recorder, equipped with mylar tape, at the ultra-low 3 ¾ rpm speed in front of the TV set, turn it on at the last minute before she left and she would have most of the two-hour show on tape when she got back. She'd have no picture record of course, but the tape would be basis enough for a discussion of your performance, and you would never know she had not loyally sat up watching you.

"It was only when she suddenly, impulsively, shot and killed her husband that the tape took on new importance. Now it was her alibi. Where is it, Inez? You must have kept it—it's your memory, so to speak, of what you didn't hear and must prove you did."

"Well, anyway," said brother Frank, reassuring himself, "Eulie's not mixed up in it at all."

She had been bent despairingly over her hands. Now she straightened up and slapped him as hard as she could in the face, and that was fairly hard.

"I mixed up in it?" she yelled. "You know what Brill was to me. I damn well *am* mixed up in it. And this filthy bitch—"

Frank's hand moved fast from his stinging face to his sister's wrist, and held it. He muttered something to her.

"I'm getting out of here," said Kim determinedly, and got up.

For the first time I looked critically at the others. Archie had an arm around his wife, and she had a handkerchief to her eyes. Twit-Twit was frowning thoughtfully. Eulalia was pulling at her brother's hand to free herself. Cohen was saying, "I'm afraid, Miss Winter—"

Kim said, "If you think I am going to let myself get involved in some cheap murder case—"

What made it so shocking was that Eulalia did not utter a sound.

She sprang, silent as a panther intent on the kill, tearing away from Frank, and launched herself at Kim, claw-like hands extended. They missed Kim's face but they found her throat, ripped her dress a little and there was a fiery spray of beads or jewels in a shower to the floor. Kim screamed, then clawed back.

"*Involved*!" cried Eulalia. "You?"

But Cohen had her. He was good at it, businesslike without being rough. He turned her back to her brother. "You're not leaving at the moment," he told Kim. Everyone picked up beads from the broken necklace and gave them to Kim. When they were all cupped in her hands, she laughed and dropped them pointedly into an ashtray. Her laugh was a metallic, humorless sound. Inez laughed too, understanding.

"You're right," Inez said. "He never was worth anything. Certainly not tearing a dress over."

Mary Sinclair raised her chin. Her cheeks were wet. "Then why did you have to kill him?" she asked, and I remembered what Archie had said about loneliness.

Kim said, "Since I can't leave, maybe you will explain something." She was addressing me. "Why would Inez kill Brill on a sudden impulse and drag his body out to Rockland County like Jersey did?"

"She didn't," I said. "I haven't come to the important part of the evidence. We know that Brillhart was going out to Rockland County and it's at least a fair assumption that Inez would go with him, considering their partnership. Perhaps he figured that the presence of his wife would help him win the Gammers over to his side in the suit.

"In any case we also know he was shot around eleven o'clock, and that it happened in his car as the bullet holes both in the car and in his body indicated. Now, Mr. Dolan and I learned tonight that some days ago the Gammers had a pair of visitors and one of them was a woman. The other certainly was Brillhart. The woman could have been Inez. Whoever they were, they left Manhattan around eight-thirty p.m., and they had a definite appointment, according to Eulalia. Therefore, they presumably knew how to find where they were going, unlike Mr. Dolan and myself tonight. Give them time to get there, talk things over, and start back for town, and it could well be a little after eleven when Brillhart is shot, killed, and dumped where he was found. Everything fits.

"But now—remember, they are on their way back to New York. Brillhart is killed in that car on a lonely road. How and why? The how is easy—he would naturally have brought along a gun, for he'd be wary of the Gammers, regardless of how the appointment was made. But *why* was he suddenly killed? If his passenger was indeed Inez, they were engaged in a mutually profitable enterprise, regardless of personal feelings. And anyway, whoever the passenger was, what agency could suddenly provoke murder? Something suddenly intruded itself in a solitary car on a dark country road late at night that caused a mortal quarrel. What did? Want to guess?"

No one did.

"The car radio," Cohen suddenly burst out.

"Sure," I said. "And you thought of it here quicker than I did. When it finally occurred to me I obtained the help of Mr. Dolan in getting a transcript of a theatrical and Hollywood gossip column-of-the-air broadcast by Belle Watkins which was on the air that night. Sure enough, she had broadcast an item to the effect that Brillhart was divorcing his wife to marry Eulalia Pope. Thus, after helping him in his blackmail attack on the Jersey estate in the hope of getting some money of her own, Inez learned dramatically that she had been double-crossed and might not be his wife by the time a settlement was made. It was a typical Brillhart tactic, of course, and her reaction was typical of her. Right, Inez?"

Again there was silence. Cohen said, "Care to say anything, Miss Low?" There was more silence.

Palpable, thick, waiting silence.

Her face was old and hopeless. Her lips opened to say *no* and froze on it.

Cohen got to his feet. "This is most interesting and I must say helpful," he said crisply. "But unofficial and informal, I'm afraid. It is necessary for several of you to drop over to the bureau for written statements, if you don't mind. You, Miss Low. And Miss Twickenham, please. And Mr. Deacon. And—"

Inez was on her feet, clutching her housecoat to herself. "I can change, can't I?" She muttered it to Cohen but she looked at me.

"Naturally." Cohen would always be courteous. But careful. "You won't mind if one of the other ladies accompanies you, will you?"

"I'll leave the door open," she said contemptuously. She walked through, then opened the door elaborately. She smiled a dark, fierce smile of dying triumph. "None of you know what he was really like," she said vindictively. "Your grief is pathetic. He was really a beast."

The broad, flowered-flannel back turned and swayed into the bedroom. Eulalia picked up scissors from an end table and lunged.

Archie, sitting on the floor, did the unexpected. He reached out and tripped Eulalia. She fell heavily, the scissors skittering away from her across the floor. Cohen and brother Frank picked her up.

Sometimes you find you have made, in a part of a second, a decision that affects a life and a death.

Brother Frank spoke soothing words to Eulalia. No one else had anything to say. I don't know what they were thinking. I know what I was. From the bedroom's open door came no sound.

Then a gun roared.

Cohen was first in. I was behind him. She lay on the bed, the gun barrel still pointed to her ear, still curling smoke. Her left hand held a roll of recording tape on her breast.

It was her confession.

Cohen was white. I suppose I was as white as Cohen.

He said, "Could you dream—?"

"Of course not. Who could have thought she'd do a thing like that?"

The others were outside the door. Twit-Twit was a frightened round-eyed child. "She's not dead?"

"Yes. The murder gun, evidently."

I ignored everyone else and put my arm around her and she began to cry unobtrusively. I wondered whether it was nervousness, or relief, or the inevitable shock of death.

Or because she had just heard me tell a somewhat obvious lie to Cohen.

# CHAPTER 3

*Twit-Twit*

We finally got to her apartment building.

"Why don't you come in for a nightcap?" said Twit-Twit. Infrequently, she becomes a little transparent. Heaven be praised.

"Well, all right."

While she fumbled in her purse for her key, I turned and looked back along the street. It was dark, except where the street lights made little worlds of light. Cars lined it, and old houses, some of them rather elegant in the restrained way of the East Sixties. There was no human being in sight; only emptiness and quiet, and a kind of peace. No more problems. It was a beautiful, dark, settled street.

Then Twit-Twit had the door open, and we went in. But I turned back, happily, to look once more. Of course, I'd see it again, later. Much later. By then the time would be well into the afternoon, and the street would be busier.

It would be nice then too.

www.ingramcontent.com/pod-product-compliance
Lightning Source LLC
Chambersburg PA
CBHW050747250626
47155CB00005B/1959